P9-CDI-623

white as silence, red as song

white as silence, red as song

ALESSANDRO D'AVENIA

THOMAS NELSON
Since 1798

White as Silence, Red as Song

Bianca Come il Latte, Rossa Come il Sangue

First published in Italian in 2010 by Mondadori.

Published in Nashville, Tennessee, by Thomas Nelson. Thomas Nelson is a registered trademark of HarperCollins Christian Publishing, Inc.

Author is represented by Andrew Nurnberg Associates Limited of 20–23, Greville Street, London EC1N 8SS.

Interior design by Mallory Collins.

Translated by Tabitha Sowden.

Thomas Nelson titles may be purchased in bulk for educational, business, fund-raising, or sales promotional use. For information, please email SpecialMarkets@ThomasNelson.com.

978-0-7852-1707-7 (ebook)

Library of Congress Cataloging-in-Publication Data

Names: D'Avenia, Alessandro, 1977- author. | Sowden, Tabitha translator.
Title: White as silence, red as song / Alessandro D'Avenia ; [translated by Tabitha Sowden].
Other titles: Biana come il latte, rossa come il sangue. English
Description: Thomas Nelson : Nashville, Tennessee, 2018.
Identifiers: LCCN 2018014520 | ISBN 9780785217060 (hard cover)
Classification: LCC PQ4904.A588 B5313 2018 | DDC 853/.92--dc23 LC record available at https://lccn.loc.gov/2018014520

Printed in the United States of America

18 19 20 21 22 LSC 5 4 3 2 1

To my parents,
who taught me to look at the sky
with my feet on the ground.

To my students,
who show me every day how to begin again.

A king's son was eating at the dinner table. While slicing the ricotta, he cut his finger, and a drop of blood fell on the white cheese. He said to his mother, "Mamma, I would like a wife white like milk and red like blood."

"Why, my son, whoever is white is certainly not red, and whoever is red is by no means white. But go out all the same and see if you can find such a girl."

Italo Calvino,

"The Love of the Three Pomegranates"

Everything is a color. Every emotion is a color.

Silence is white—and I can't stand white. It has no boundaries: a white elephant, a white flag, a white lie . . . In fact, white isn't even a color. It is nothing, like silence. A kind of nothing without words or music. Silent, alone. I can't be silent or alone, which are the same thing. I feel a pain just above my stomach—or inside my stomach, I've never quite worked it out—that compels me to jump on my run-down Batscooter without brakes (when will I get around to fixing it?) and ride aimlessly, staring at girls in the street to determine if I am alone. If any one of them stares back at me, I exist.

But why am I like this? I lose control. I don't know how to be alone. I need . . . even I don't know what. It drives me crazy! So I have an iPod instead. Because when you know that the day ahead will taste like dusty tarmac at school, followed by a tunnel of boredom, homework, parents, and dog, over and over again until death do us part, the only thing that can save you is the right soundtrack. With a pair of headphones in your ears, you enter another dimension. You get into the right color mood. If I need to fall in love: melodic rock. If I need to recharge: pure heavy metal. If I need to pump myself up:

rap and various kinds of profanities. That way I'm not alone. White. Someone is there to give color to my day.

Not that I get bored. Theoretically I have thousands of ideas, ten thousand plans, a million dreams to fulfill, a billion projects to start. But I can't seem to start a single one because nobody's interested. So I end up asking myself, *Leo, who the hell are you doing this for? Forget it and enjoy what you have.*

There is only one life, and when it turns white, my computer is the best way to color it. I always find someone to chat with. (My nickname is Pirate, like Captain Jack Sparrow.) Because listening to others is something I can do. It makes me feel good. Or I get on my Batscooter without brakes and ride around. If I do have a destination, it's to go to Niko's and play a few tunes together, him on the bass guitar and me on the electric guitar. We'll be famous one day. We'll have our own band and we'll call it The Crew. Niko says I should sing too because I have a good voice, but I'm shy. When you play the guitar your fingers do the singing, and fingers never blush. Nobody boos a guitarist, whereas a singer . . .

If Niko is busy, I meet the others at the bus stop. It's the stop outside school, the one where every single infatuated guy has declared his love to the world. There is always someone hanging out there, sometimes girls too. Sometimes even Beatrice is there, and that's why I go. For her.

It's weird how nobody wants to go to school in the morning but then everyone hangs out there in the afternoon. The difference is that the vampires—the teachers, that is—have left. The bloodsuckers go home in the afternoon and crawl back into their sarcophaguses waiting for their next victims. Though, unlike vampires, teachers act during the day.

But if Beatrice is at the bus stop, everything is different. When her green eyes are wide open, they fill her entire face. When she lets down her red hair, it feels like the sunrise has smothered you. She has few words, carefully chosen. If she were a movie, she'd be a genre not yet invented. If she were a scent, she'd be early morning sand, when the beach is alone with the sea. Color? Beatrice is red. The way love is red. A tempest. A hurricane that sweeps you away. An earthquake that crumbles your body to pieces. That's how I feel every time I see her. She doesn't know yet, but one of these days I'll tell her.

Yes, one of these days I'll tell her that she is the one for me and I am the one for her. That's the way it is, and there's no getting away from it. When she realizes it, everything will be perfect, like in the movies. I just have to find the right moment and the right hairstyle. I think it's mostly a problem of hair. I would only cut it if Beatrice asked me to. But what if I lose my strength like the guy in that story? No, a Pirate shouldn't cut his hair, and a lion without a mane is not a lion. There's a reason my name is Leo.

I once saw a documentary about lions. A male lion with a huge mane appeared out of the brush as a gentle voice-over said, "The king of the forest has his crown." That's what my hair is like. Free and majestic.

A lion's mane is easy to look after. I never have to comb it—just let it grow wild, as if every strand is a thought bursting out of my head, occasionally exploding and spraying out, like the exhilarating fizz that Coke makes when you first open a can. I give my thoughts to others and say a lot with my hair. It's so true. What I've just said is so true.

People understand me *because of* my hair. Well, at least, the others in the group do, the other Pirates: Sponge, Beanpole, and Curly. Dad gave up ages ago. Mom does nothing but criticize me. Nan nearly dies of heart failure whenever she sees me, but that's no big deal if you're ninety.

Why do they find it so difficult to understand my hair? First they say, "You have to be original. Express yourself! Be yourself!" Then, when you try to show who you really are, they say, "You have no identity. You behave like all the others!" What kind of logic is that? I just don't get it. You're either yourself or you're like everyone else. Either way, they're never happy. The truth is, they're envious. Especially the baldies. If I ever go bald I'll kill myself.

Anyhow, if Beatrice doesn't like my hair, I guess I'll cut it—but I want to think about it, as it could also be a strong point. Beatrice, either you love me the way I am, with this hair, or we're going nowhere. If we don't agree on the little things, how can we ever be together? We have to be ourselves and accept others as they are—that's what they always say on TV—otherwise, what kind of love is it? Come on, Beatrice. Why don't you get it? And anyway, I already like everything about you, so you have a head start. Girls are always ahead. How is it they always win? If you're pretty, you have the entire world at your feet. You choose what you want, do what you want, wear what you want . . . Nothing matters because everyone looks up to you anyway. How lucky!

Me, on the other hand, I have days when I don't even want to leave the house. I feel so ugly I just want to hide in my room, never looking at myself in the mirror. White. With a white face. Colorless. What torture. But then there are days when I am red too. Where do you find a guy like me? I throw on the right T-shirt, pull up my jeans till they sit just perfectly, and feel like a god. Zac Efron, eat your heart out. I go out on my own. I could quite happily say to the first girl I come across, "Hey, gorgeous. Let's go out tonight. Seize the incredible opportunity I'm offering you! If you're with me, everyone will look at you and say, 'How on earth did you manage to hook up with a guy like him? Your girlfriends will be green with envy!' "

I'm a hero! I have such a full life. I never stop. If it weren't for school, I'd already be someone.

If I didn't have to go to school, I would probably be more rested, handsome, and famous. My school is called Horace, like the Mickey Mouse character. The walls are peeling, and the classrooms have blackboards that are more gray than black, as well as frayed maps with continents and nations that have long faded or gone adrift. The walls are painted two colors, white and brown, like an ice cream sandwich. But there is nothing nice about school except the dismissal bell. And when it starts its incessant ringing, it seems to be screaming out at you, "Run for it! You've wasted another day inside these two-colored walls!"

On rare occasions, school is useful—like when I suddenly feel down and I'm drowning in white thoughts, asking myself where I'm going, what I'm doing, if I'll ever do anything positive with my life, if . . . Fortunately, the playground is full of people in the same situation as me. We talk about everything; we let go of the kinds of thoughts that ultimately lead to nothing. White thoughts lead to nothing, so white thoughts must be eliminated.

In a McDonald's that smells of McDonald's, I devour hot French fries while Niko noisily slurps his huge Coke through a straw.

You mustn't think of white.

Niko is always telling me that. Niko is always right. There's a reason he's my best friend. He is like Will Turner to Jack Sparrow. We save each other's lives at least once a month because that's what friends are for. Me, I choose my friends. That's the good thing about friends. You choose them and you feel good with them because you choose the ones you want. Whereas you don't choose your classmates. They just happen to you, and sometimes they are a real pain in the neck.

Niko is in form B—I'm in D—and we play on the same five-a-side soccer team at school: the Pirates. A pair of soccer wunderkinds. There's someone in class who's constantly nervous named Electra. The name says it all. Some people condemn their kids with the choice of a name. I'm called Leo and I'm cool with that. I was lucky: The name makes you think of someone strong and attractive stepping out of the forest like a lion with a mane. Roaring. Or, at least in my case, trying to. Unfortunately, everyone's fate is sealed in their name. Take Electra. What kind of name is that? It sounds like electric current, and the name alone is enough to give you a shock. That's why she's always on edge.

There's always a professional ball-breaker too: Giacomo—known as Stinker—is another name that brings bad luck! It makes one think of Giacomo Leopardi, who was a poet with a hunchback and no friends. Nobody speaks to Giacomo. He smells. And nobody has the courage to tell him. Since I've fallen in love with Beatrice, I shower every day and shave once a month. At the end of the day it's Giacomo's problem if he doesn't bathe, though surely at least his mother could say something about it. But no. Anyway, it's not my fault. I can't save the world. Spiderman can see to that.

Niko's burp brings me back to earth, and in between fits of laughter I say to him, "You're right. I mustn't think about white."

Niko slaps me on the back. "I want to see you all hyped up tomorrow! We've got to put those losers to shame!" I beam with delight. What would school be like without the soccer tournament?

"I don't know why I did it, I don't know why I enjoyed it, and I don't know why I'll do it again": my life philosophy summarized in a Bart Simpson quote. Bart is my sole teacher and guide. Today our history and philosophy teacher is sick. Yay! We'll get a substitute teacher. She'll be the usual loser.

You mustn't say that!

Mom's threatening words ring out in my head, but I say it anyway. When needs must! A substitute teacher is by definition a concentration of cosmic loser.

Firstly: because substitute teachers sit in for regular teachers, who are already losers—meaning a substitute teacher is three times a loser.

Secondly: just for being a substitute teacher. What kind of life is that—taking over for someone who's sick?

That is, not only are substitutes losers, but also they bring bad luck to others. Loser to the nth degree. A loser is purple, because purple is the color of death.

We wait for her to arrive. She'll be ugly with an immaculate purple dress, and we'll pummel her with saliva-drenched paper pellets fired with utmost precision from empty Bic pens.

Instead, a young guy walks in wearing a shirt and jacket.

Neat. Eyes too dark for my liking. Dark glasses too resting on his nose, which is too long. A bagful of books. He goes on about how he loves what he studies. That's all we need, someone who believes in it. They're the worst! I can't remember his name. He told us, but I was busy talking to Silvia. Silvia is the kind of person you can talk to about anything. I'm really fond of her and I often hug her. I do it because she's happy and so am I. But she's not my type. I mean, she's cool, you can talk to her about anything, and she knows how to listen and give you advice. But she doesn't have that extra something: the magic, the charm. What Beatrice has. She doesn't have Beatrice's red hair. Beatrice just needs to look at you to make you dream. Beatrice is red. Silvia is blue, like all real friends. Whereas this substitute teacher is just a tiny black stain on a hopelessly white day!

Loser, loser, super-loser!

He has dark hair. Dark eyes. A dark jacket. Basically he looks like the Death Star in *Star Wars*. All he's missing is killer breath with which to put an end to students and colleagues. He doesn't know what to do because he hasn't been given instructions, and no one can reach Mrs. Argentieri on her cell phone. Mrs. Argentieri has a cell phone but doesn't even know how to use it. Her children gave it to her. It even has a camera, but she doesn't have a clue. She just uses it to call her husband. Because her husband is sick. He has cancer, poor guy! Tons of people get cancer. If it gets to your liver, that's it. Really bad deal. Her husband has liver cancer.

Mrs. Argentieri never spoke to us about it. We learned about it from our PE teacher, Mrs. Nicolosi. Her husband is a doctor, and Mrs. Argentieri's husband takes chemo at the hospital where Mrs. Nicolosi's husband works. Jeez, Mrs. Argentieri has been so unlucky! She's tedious and fussy as hell, obsessed with that guy who said you can't step twice into the same river—which seems pretty obvious to me. But I feel sorry for her when she checks her phone to see if her husband has called.

Anyhow, the substitute teacher tries to teach us, but—like

all substitute teachers—he has no shot because, quite rightly, no one pays any attention. In fact, it's a great opportunity to mess around and have a laugh at the expense of a grown-up's failure. At one point I raise my hand and ask him, in a serious voice, "Why did you choose this job?"

And in a whisper I add, "As a loser?"

Everyone laughs. He's unfazed.

"Because of my granddad."

This guy is nuts.

"When I was ten years old, my grandfather told me the story of *A Thousand and One Nights*."

Silence.

"But let's talk about the Carolingian Renaissance now."

The entire class looks at me. I am the one who started it, and I have to continue. They're right. I am their hero.

"Excuse me, sir, but do you mean the story of *A Thousand and* . . . well, that one?"

Somebody chuckles. Silence. A rolling tumbleweed, Wild West type of silence. His eyes meet my eyes.

"I presumed you weren't interested in how to become a loser."

Silence. He's got the upper hand. I don't know what to say.

"No, in fact, we're not interested."

But in reality I am interested. I want to know why someone dreams about becoming a loser, then works hard for that dream to come true. He even seems happy. The others glare at me. Not even Silvia approves.

"Do tell us, sir. We're interested," she says.

Abandoned even by Silvia, I turn to white as the teacher begins, with those devilish eyes of his.

"Mohamed el-Magrebi lived in Cairo, in a little house with a garden, a fig tree, and a fountain. He was poor. He fell asleep and dreamed of a drenched man who removed a golden coin from his mouth and said to him, 'Your fortune is in Persia. You will find a treasure in Isfahan . . . so you must go there!' Mohamed awoke and set off immediately. After encountering a thousand dangers he reached Isfahan. Here, as he tried to find food, exhausted, he was mistaken for a thief. He was beaten almost to death with bamboo sticks. Later the chief of police asked him, 'Who are you, where are you from, why are you here?' The man told him the truth: 'I dreamed of a drenched man who told me to come here because I would find a treasure. Yet all I've gotten is a beating!' The chief of police chuckled and replied, 'Idiot. You believe in dreams? Three times I dreamt about a humble house in Cairo with a garden, a fig tree, and a fountain, and beneath the fountain a huge treasure! But I never set off to find it! Away with you, you sucker!' The man returned home, dug beneath the fountain in his garden, and found the treasure!"

He tells the story with the right pauses, like an actor. My classmates are all wide-eyed and dumbstruck. This is a bad sign. All we needed was a storytelling substitute teacher. I greet the end of the story with a chuckle.

"Is that it?"

The substitute teacher stands up without saying a word. He sits on the desk.

"That's it. That day my granddad explained to me that we are different from animals. Animals can only follow their natural instincts. We, on the other hand, are free. It's the greatest gift we've ever received. Thanks to our freedom, we can become something different from what we are. Freedom allows us to dream, and dreams are the blood of life, even if that occasionally means taking a long journey and getting a bit beaten up along the way. 'Never give up on your dreams! Don't be frightened of dreaming even if others laugh at you,' my granddad told me. 'You would be giving up on yourself.' I still remember the shine in his eyes as he said those words."

Everyone is silent, in awe, and it annoys me that this guy is the center of attention when I'm supposed to be the center of attention whenever we have substitute teachers.

"What does this have to do with history and philosophy, sir?"

He stares at me.

"History is a cauldron of projects undertaken by people who became great for having the courage to turn their dreams into reality, and philosophy is the silence from which these dreams are born. Even if at times, unfortunately, the dreams these men had were nightmares, especially to those who paid the price. When they're not born out of silence, dreams become nightmares. History, together with philosophy, art, music, and literature, is the best way of discovering and understanding humanity. Alexander the Great, Caesar Augustus, Dante, Michelangelo . . . Men who challenged themselves and, by *changing* themselves, changed history. Perhaps the next Dante or Michelangelo is right here in this classroom. Perhaps it could be you!"

The teacher's eyes shine as he talks about the actions of ordinary people who became great thanks to their dreams, thanks to their freedom. I'm bowled over, but even more bowled over by the fact that I'm actually listening to this jerk.

"Only when people have faith in what is beyond their reach—a dream—does humanity take steps forward that help it to believe in itself." Not a bad point, though it does seem to be the obvious thing a young, idealistic teacher would say. I'd like to see where he and his dreams end up in a year's time! That's why I nickname him The Dreamer. Good for him that he has dreams and believes in them.

"Sir, it seems to me like all talk."

I want to work out whether he is serious or has simply built himself a world with which to cover up his life as a loser. The Dreamer looks me in the eye and after a moment's silence says:

"What are you afraid of?"

Then the bell saves my thoughts, suddenly turned white and silent.

Me, I'm not scared of anything. I'm in the third year at a classics high school. It's where my parents wanted me to go. I didn't have a clue what I wanted. Mom studied classics. Dad studied classics. Nan is the embodiment of classics. Only our dog was spared.

It opens your mind, expands your horizons, structures your brain, makes you flexible . . .

And breaks your balls from dawn till dusk.

That's exactly how it is. There's not a single valid reason to go to this kind of school. At least the teachers have never provided one. First day of the first year: presentations, tour of the building, introduction to the teachers. Like a field trip to the zoo where the teachers are a kind of endangered species that you hope will become permanently extinct.

Next come a few entrance tests to determine the starting level of each student. And after this warm welcome, pure hell: We're reduced to shadows and dust. Homework, explanations, and tests like I'd never seen before. In middle school I'd study half an hour at most. Then off to play soccer anywhere that could remotely pass as a field, from the corridor at home to the parking lot downstairs. Lacking that, soccer on the PlayStation.

Things are different in high school. If you want to pass the year, you have to study. I still don't study much, though, because you only do things if you believe in them. And no teacher ever managed to convince me it is worth it. And if they—who dedicate their life to study—cannot convince me, why should I do it?

I read The Dreamer's blog. Yes, the history and philosophy substitute teacher has a blog, and I was curious to see what he writes on it. Teachers don't have lives outside school. They don't *exist* outside school. So I wanted to see what somebody who has nothing to talk about actually talks about. He talked about a movie he'd seen for the millionth time: *Dead Poets Society*. He said he shared the same passion for teaching as the protagonist of the film. He said the film had shown him why he was on earth. He continued with a mysterious yet beautiful sentence: "To grasp beauty from anywhere and share it with those beside me. That's why I'm here."

I must say, The Dreamer knows how to put things into words. Two sentences and you can tell he's worked his life out. I mean, he is thirty already, so obviously he's worked it out. But people don't always manage to say things so clearly. He figured out his dream when he was my age. Then he set his goal and reached it.

I'm sixteen and don't have any special dreams, other than those I have when I'm sleeping and never remember in the morning. Erika-with-a-*k* believes that dreams depend on reincarnation, on what we were in our previous life. Like the soccer player who claims he was a duck in his previous life, which improved his soccer skills. Erika-with-a-*k* says she was a jasmine plant. That's why she always smells nice. I like the smell of Erika-with-a-*k*.

I don't think I've ever been reincarnated. But if I could choose, I think I'd prefer an animal to a plant: a lion, a tiger, a scorpion. Sure, the whole reincarnation thing is a problematic idea, but it's too complex to think about now, and anyhow I have no memory of being a lion, even if I've still got a mane and can feel the strength of a lion running through my veins. That's why I must have been a lion, and that's why I'm called Leo. *Leo* means "lion" in Latin. *Leo rugens*: "roaring lion."

Anyhow, I'm in the third year of a classics high school, and I got through the first and second years almost unscathed. First year I had to retake ancient Greek and math. Second year just Greek. Ancient Greek is a school equivalent of your daily greens: tasteless and only good for aiding digestion.

Ms. Massaroni was to blame. She's the fussiest and most ruthless teacher in school. She wears a dog fur coat, day in and day out, constantly. She has two outfits: a dog fur coat for winter, fall, and spring. And another dog fur coat for summer. What kind of life is that? Perhaps she was a dog in her previous life. I enjoy giving people a former life in my head. It helps explain their character.

Beatrice, for instance, must have been a star in her previous life. Because stars have a blinding luminosity around them. You can spot them a million light-years away. They are clusters of bright, incandescent, red material. And that's Beatrice. You can spot her from a hundred yards. She emanates red. I wonder if I'll ever kiss her. By the way, it's her birthday soon. She might invite me to her party. I'll go to the school bus stop today to see her. Beatrice is red wine. She makes me drunk: I love her.

When you have a tournament in the afternoon, there's no time for anything else. You have to prepare yourself mentally and savor the excitement. Every gesture becomes important and must be perfect. My favorite moment is when you pull up your sports socks: like a piece of ancient armor or the greaves of a medieval knight, they slowly caress your shins.

Our opponents today are from 4B. A school full of rich kids. We need to thrash them. Pirates against Smartarses. The outcome is certain, but not the number of victims. We'll purge as many as possible. The third-generation synthetic soccer field tickles every inch of my body. Our red T-shirts, with the image of a skull above the word *Pirates*, stand out in this warm fall afternoon. We're all here: Niko, Curly, Beanpole, and Sponge—who looks more like an armored door than a goalie. We've got the right attitude. That makes the difference. The others are full of pimples and look more like losers than smartarses.

They barely have a chance to realize who they're dealing with before we've already made two goals. Niko scores one and I score the other. True pirates of the penalty area. One always knows where the other is, even with our eyes closed, back-to-back, like brothers. As I celebrate my evil and well-placed shot, I notice Silvia watching the match with her girlfriends: Erika-with-a-*k*, Electra, Leggy, Eli, Fra, and Barbie. They are chatting among themselves. Like they always do. Girls don't give a flip about the match. Only Silvia cheers for my goal. And I blow her a kiss, like great soccer players do to thank their fans. One day Beatrice will be there to blow me a kiss. I will dedicate my best goal to her, and I will run toward the crowd showing everyone my T-shirt with "I belong to Beatrice" written on it.

Mrs. Argentieri's husband has died. We won't be seeing her again; she's decided to retire early. She's devastated. Sure, she has two children taking care of her, but her husband was her reason for living. Certainly not history and philosophy anymore. We get to keep The Dreamer. Substitute teachers definitely jinx things . . . Husbands have to die for them to get a job.

Anyhow, we have to go to the husband's funeral, and I really don't know how to deal with these things. I don't know what to wear. Silvia, the only woman I trust when it comes to style, tells me I have to wear dark clothes, like a blue sweater and shirt. Jeans are okay, given that I don't have proper pants. There are tons of people from school in the church. I sit toward the back because I have no idea when I'm supposed to stand or sit. And what if I bump into Mrs. Argentieri? What are you supposed to say in these situations? The word *condolences*—is that how you pronounce it?—sounds vulgar to me. Better to be inconspicuous. I can blend in with the crowd, invisible and insignificant.

The funeral is conducted by the priest, who is also my religious studies teacher: Gandalf, with his tiny, almost pocket-size body and millions of fine, lively wrinkles—because of which everyone at school calls him Gandalf, like the wizard in the Lord of the Rings.

Mrs. Argentieri is sitting in the front row, black on the outside, white on the inside. She is drying her tears with a handkerchief, and her children are sitting next to her: a man around forty and a younger, reasonable-looking woman. Teachers' children are always a mystery because you never know if they have ordinary kids. Teachers probably spend all day teaching them! It must be awful.

But Mrs. Argentieri is crying and I'm sorry about it. At the end of the service our paths cross—accidentally—and she looks at me as if expecting something. I smile. It's the only thing I can do. She looks down and walks out behind the wooden coffin. I'm such a pirate. The woman has just lost her husband and all I can do is smile. I feel bad. Perhaps I could have said something. But I just don't know how to behave in certain situations. Am I to blame?

Back home I don't feel like doing anything. I'd like to be alone, but I can't stand the white. I put on some music and get online. I chat to Niko about the funeral.

Where is the husband now?

Has he been reincarnated?

Has he turned to ash?

Is he suffering?

I hope he's not suffering anymore because he has already suffered a lot. Niko doesn't know. He thinks there is something after life. But he definitely doesn't want to be reincarnated as a fly. Why a fly? He says it's because at home he's constantly told he's as annoying as a fly.

Speaking of which—actually, it's not really related—but I *can't* forget Beatrice's birthday. In fact, I'll send her a text message now: "Hi, Beatrice, it's Leo, the guy from third year with wild hair. It's your birthday soon. Do you have any plans? Talk to you later, Leo §:-)." She doesn't reply. I feel stupid. What must Beatrice think now? That I'm the usual loser who strikes out via text message? The silence fills my heart, like a painter preparing to whitewash a surface, erasing Beatrice's name with a uniform layer of white. Pain, fear, and loneliness radiate from my silent phone and rip out my insides . . .

First the funeral, then Beatrice not answering. Two white doors closing in front of me and, what's more, bearing the phrase "Do not block." The doors are not only shutting me out but also telling me to get out of the way. Don't think about it. But how?

I call Silvia. We spend two hours on the phone. She knows that I just need someone to talk to, and she says so. She gets me instantly, even when I talk about other things. Silvia must have been an angel in her previous life. She's quick to grasp things, and apparently that's what angels are like. It's why they have wings. At least that's what The Sister (Anna, our über-Catholic classmate) says: "Everyone has a guardian angel beside them. All you need to do is tell angels what is happening to you, and they will immediately understand." I don't believe it. But I do believe Silvia is my guardian angel. I feel relieved. She opened those doors again. We say good night and I fall asleep peacefully, because I can always talk to her. I hope Silvia will always be there, even when we are grown up. But I'm still in love with Beatrice.

Just before falling asleep I check my phone. A message! It must be Beatrice's reply. I'm saved. "If you can't sleep, I'm here. S." How I wish that the *S* were a *B*.

Give me a motorbike, even just a Batscooter, and I will lift up the world. Yes, because there is nothing better than riding past school and seeing Beatrice there with her friends. I don't have the nerve to stop, since she might tell me in front of everybody that she doesn't want to get any more of my loser messages. So I just ride past with my hair flapping in the wind beneath my helmet and shoot her a Cupid's arrow look. That's enough to give me a boost. Yes, because without that boost I would feel depressed and have to call Silvia to talk about other things. Is there anyone you can talk to about the hard things?

Thankfully the red-beamed star turns to look at me. She knows it was me who wrote that message, and her look reassures me that there is still a reason to live. I'm saved!

I sail along on my scooter, passing a million traffic-jammed cars as if they aren't even there. All the air in the world caresses my face, and I take it all in as one takes in freedom. I sing out, "You're the first thought that wakes me in the morning," and when I finally come to my senses, it's already dark.

I've roamed about aimlessly on my flying carpet, without noticing the time passing. When you're in love, time shouldn't exist. But my mother exists. She's not in love with Beatrice, and she's furious because she had no idea where I was. What can I do about it? It's love. The red bits of life are like that: timeless.

"What were you thinking?" she says.

Grown-ups can't remember what it's like to be in love. What's the point in explaining something to someone who no longer remembers it? What's the point in describing red to a blind person? Mom doesn't understand, and what's more, she wants me to take Terminator out to pee every day.

Terminator is our retired dachshund. He eats, slides around on his elongated belly, and pees hundreds of gallons. I only take him out to pee when I don't feel like doing my homework; then he can pee for hours on end while I use the opportunity to look at girls and window shop. Why do people buy dogs? Perhaps to provide work for cleaning ladies who then have to take them out for walks. Parks are full of cleaning ladies with dogs. But if you don't have a cleaning lady you're screwed, like me. Anyway, pets are just stand-ins. Terminator only knows how to pee. Life as a dog.

I can't sleep. I'm in love, and when you're in love, the very least that happens to you is not sleeping. Even the blackest night can turn red. So much stuff fills your brain, you want to think about all of it at the same time and your heart is restless. And it's strange because everything seems okay. You're living the same life, day in, day out, with the same things and the same boredom. Then you fall in love, and your life becomes great and different. You're living in the same world as Beatrice, so who cares if you get a bad grade, if your scooter tire gets punctured, if Terminator wants to pee, or if it's raining and you don't have an umbrella? You don't care, because you know that those things pass. But love doesn't. Your red star always shines. Beatrice is there, love is in your heart, and it is amazing. It makes you dream, and nobody can take the dream from you because it is somewhere nobody can reach. I don't know how to describe it: I hope it never goes away.

That's how I eventually fall asleep, with hope in my heart. As long as Beatrice is there, life starts over every day. It's love that gives new life. That's so true. I have to remember it. I forget so many important things that I have discovered. I realize they could be useful to me in the future, but then I forget them, like adults do. And that is the reason for at least half of the world's evils. "In my day, these problems didn't even exist," they say. Precisely. In *your* time!

Perhaps if I make a note somewhere of the things I learn, I won't forget them and won't make the same mistakes. I have a terrible memory. It's my parents' fault: dodgy DNA. There's only one thing I haven't forgotten: five-a-side soccer tournament tomorrow.

That's not true. There's something else I haven't forgotten: Beatrice never replied to my message. There's no hope for me. Shroud me in white, like a mummy.

Gandalf is a man made of wind. He gives the impression he could fly away any minute like a balloon, and you wonder how he manages to put up with hordes of barbaric schoolkids. Yet he is always smiling. He has scattered his smiles along the school's marble floors. When you bump into him he smiles, even when he arrives at school, unlike the other teachers. It almost seems like that smile doesn't belong to him.

He walks into class, smiles, and says nothing. We all wait for the moment when he writes a sentence on the blackboard. Today he walks in and writes, "For where your treasure is, there your heart will be also."

The usual game starts.

"Jovanotti!"

"No."

"Max Pezzali?"

"No."

"Elisa?"

"No. Older . . ."

"Battisti?"

"No."

"I've got it!"

I shout from the back of the classroom, spreading my arms theatrically as a prelude to my triumphal moment:

"Uncle Scrooge!"

Everyone bursts out laughing.

Even Gandalf smiles and says nothing. He stares at us and says, "Jesus Christ."

"There's always a catch," I say. "You really can't live without Jesus, sir."

"Do you think I would go around dressed like this if I could live without him?" He smiles.

"But what does it mean?"

He smiles. "What do you think?"

"Like Gollum, who always talks about 'my precious.' He thinks of nothing else, so that's where his heart is," says The Sister. She doesn't say much, but when she does it's usually something profound.

"I don't know who this Gollum is, but if you say so, I trust you."

Gandalf doesn't know who Gollum is. Crazy but true. Then he continues:

"It means that when we believe we're thinking about nothing, in actual fact we're thinking about what is dear to us. Love is a kind of gravitational force: invisible and universal, just like the earth's gravity. Without us realizing it, our hearts, eyes, and words are inevitably drawn to it, like the apple to the ground."

"What if we don't love anything?"

"Impossible. Can you imagine the earth without gravity? Or space without gravity? Everything would be in constant collision. Even those who think they love nothing love something. And that's where their thoughts end up, without them even realizing it. The point is not whether we love or not, but *what* we love. Man always loves something: beauty, intelligence, money, health, God . . ."

"How can you love God if you can't touch him?"

"You can touch him."

"How?"

"You touch his body during the Eucharist."

"But, sir, that's just a way of saying it's symbolic."

"You think I've put my life at stake for a symbol? What do you love, Leo? What do you think about when you think about nothing?"

I don't say anything, as I'm too embarrassed to say it out loud. Silvia gives me the look of someone expecting to hear the right answer during an oral test, or as if wanting to give me a clue. I know the answer. I'd like to scream it to the whole world: Beatrice is my force of gravity, my weight, my blood, my red.

"I think of red."

Somebody laughs, pretending to have understood a joke I haven't actually made.

Gandalf has realized I'm not joking.

"And what kind of red is it?"

"Like her hair . . ."

The others look at me as if I've gotten high before class. The only one who seems to understand is Silvia, who gives me a knowing look.

Gandalf looks me in the eyes, or even inside my eyes. He smiles and says, "Me too."

"And what kind of red is it?"

"Like his blood."

Now it's our turn to look at him as if he's smoked a joint.

He goes to the blackboard and silently writes out, "My beloved is white and ruddy."

And the game starts over.

These are lessons with Gandalf. They are devised at the spur of the moment, and he always seems to have a phrase on hand in his magical book.

Nobody knows this one, and when he tells us it's from the Bible, nobody believes him. So we end up being given religion homework too: read the Song of Songs.

Nobody does religion homework. The only things you need to do in life are the ones that get you a grade.

There is nothing better than hanging out with Niko doing the following:

Light lunch at McDonald's, followed by a burp contest on our scooters.

A chill PlayStation session at his place: two hours of *Grand Theft Auto*. We must have massacred at least a dozen police officers with the chain saw. It gives you a massive adrenaline rush that you are forced to release onto your soccer opponents. They don't stand a chance.

Prepping for the match with homemade drugs: a banana smoothie that only Niko's mom knows the ingredients of. Niko's mom is a die-hard fan of ours, and she supplies us with banana dope.

Then, finally, it's time for the match. Today we're playing against the Fantacalcio team. They're good, they're in fifth year. We beat them last year and because of that they're fully charged, ready for revenge. You can tell by the look on Vandal's face. He's their captain. He does nothing but stare at me. He has no idea what's in store for him.

No one is there to cheer us on today. It must be because we

have a biology test tomorrow. Being sensible, I planned ahead: I decided to skip the test.

We start by warming up Sponge's rusty hands by kicking him some wicked low shots. Curly seems under the weather today. Niko and I take the lead, brimming with banana smoothie and pent-up *GTA* adrenaline. The field is waiting for our shoes to skim across it.

The match is stuck at zero-zero for the entire first half. Vandal has done nothing but break Niko's balls. He's on his back constantly. No breathing space. We need to change something we're doing, but I don't know what. All I know is that when Niko next has him nipping at his ankles like a Neapolitan bulldog, leaving him no time to think or shoot, the *GTA* adrenaline takes over and Niko hammers down on Vandal's heels, who has meanwhile managed to steal the ball from him. Vandal keels over with a cry of pain. It's a miracle if he hasn't broken a leg. He's doubled over and possessed, like Gollum. Everyone gathers around. I've barely had the chance to approach when a punch lands on Niko's nose, making him double over too, blood pouring into his hands. Without thinking twice I run up to the guy who punched Niko.

"What the hell do you think you're doing, idiot?"

The look in his eyes isn't normal. It's more of an evil glare that lunges against me like a compressed spring. A violent shove takes my breath away and throws me into the air before I land on my backside.

"What did you call me?"

I can feel his rotten breath filling my nostrils. I don't have the courage to react. It would be the end of me. At this point, fortunately, the referee finally intervenes and sends both Niko and the hotheaded brute off the field.

Without Niko the match fizzles out. Vandal recovers and scores a goal with his incontrollable anger.

When I head back to the locker room, Niko has left. Vandal is waiting for me at the exit with his thugs.

This is going to end badly.

"Your pal was lucky today. Next time he won't leave the field alive. Go and comfort him, you queer!"

The Pirate and his entire crew are reduced to the silence of defeat and humiliation by a horde of angry tyrants.

Niko has come to school with two black eyes. The guy who punched him is being suspended from the tournament.

"He'll pay for it. You've got no idea what I'll do to him. No idea . . ."

Niko is fuming.

"Come on, Niko. He was disqualified. You didn't exactly tackle him gently."

Niko glares at me with his half-closed eyes. "You're taking his side? Did you leave your balls at home?"

"If you had calmed down a bit, we wouldn't have lost yesterday—"

"Ah, so it's my fault now. Screw you, Leo."

He turns his back without giving me the chance to react. Great start to the day.

The Dreamer has walked into the classroom with a booklet in his hand. A hundred or so pages long.

"A book that will change your life," he says. I never thought that books could change anything, let alone your life. I mean, they change it in the sense that you're forced to read them when you would rather be doing something completely different. But The Dreamer is a dreamer and he can't avoid dreaming. Anyhow, what does that book have to do with history? The Dreamer told us that to understand the era we're studying, we have to truly get into the hearts of the people of that time. Then he starts to read from a Dante Alighieri book. Not *The Divine Comedy*, which is a cosmic bore. A little book, Dante's love story.

I can barely believe it: Dante has even written a book for Beatrice. He was totally in love, like me. The book is called *The New Life*. Just as I had already figured out for myself, love makes everything new. What if I could be the next Dante? What if The Dreamer were right for once? Anyhow, Dante's book is dedicated to his encounter with Beatrice and to how his life changed after that. Unbelievable. Some prehistoric guy feeling exactly the same things as me! Am I the reincarnation of Dante?

But try to tell that to Ms. Rocca, who describes my writing as "sloppy and contorted" and never gives me a grade higher than a D minus minus, which is the worst kind of fail in disguise. So I'm not the reincarnation of Dante! Though not even Dante is comprehensible now, so maybe if what I write is incomprehensible it is because I have a Dantesque future. Whatever. Even if I'm not Dante, Beatrice is still Beatrice and I can't stop thinking about her and talking about her. As Dante says, "I wish to speak with you about my lady, not because I think to end her praises, but speaking so that I can ease my mind."

Dante is always right! But I should read his book. Maybe I can copy out a few poems and dedicate them to Beatrice. Actually, I'll send her a message with a famous quote from the book. She'll surely respond to that text, because I won't come across as an idiot. She'll realize I'm serious, like Dante. I can't give up: A lion that gives up is not a lion; a pirate who retreats is not a pirate. She'll understand because she studied these things last year, and if she doesn't remember them she'll ask me. Beatrice is in fourth year. She's very clever. I send her a message: "From *Vita Nova* . . ." It sounds so cool in Latin and adds a touch of class. My T9 can't read Latin, but Beatrice will understand it.

There is just one thing that's annoying me. To the eyes of everyone, The Dreamer is coming out ahead of his loser-storyteller-jinxer persona. It's happening before my very eyes and I can't stand it. I have to do something to put him back in his place: I need to find out his weak spot and launch a Pirate attack . . .

T9 is the twenty-first-century invention. It saves you a load of time and also makes you chuckle when you want to write a word and it thinks you want to write something else that means something completely different. For instance, when you have to write "sorry," the word that comes up first is "soppy." It's really quite a coincidence because when I have to apologize for something I really do feel a bit soppy.

I like predictive text. I wonder if Dante had something like T9 to help him write all that prose. It's hard to understand how some people can do what they do. They must be destined for it. I don't know how to do anything well yet, but I'm hopeful. My English teacher says I "have the skills but don't apply them." That's me: I have the skills, I could do anything, but I haven't decided to take things seriously yet. I could be Dante, Michelangelo, Einstein, Eminem, or Jovanotti. I still don't know which one. I should try to find out.

According to The Dreamer I need to find my dream, then turn it into a project. I should ask him how you find out what your dream is. I would ask him, but I'm embarrassed and would end up agreeing with him . . . And anyway, this obsession about having a dream when you're just sixteen doesn't really convince me. Whatever the case, I'm absolutely positive that Beatrice fits into it somewhere.

Speaking of Beatrice, she didn't answer my text, and I'm upset because I thought Dante would impress her. My stomach clenches and my heart turns white. As if Beatrice herself wanted to delete me from the face of the earth with Wite-Out. I feel like a mistake. A spelling mistake. A misplaced apostrophe or a redundant letter. A drop of Wite-Out and I will disappear like any old typo. The sheet of paper becomes crisp and clean again, and nobody can see the pain hidden behind that layer of white.

Poetry is garbage in rhyme. Take that, Dante!

Beatrice has red hair. Beatrice has green eyes. Beatrice has.

In the afternoons she hangs out with her friends outside school. She's not dating anyone. I went to her birthday party last year, and it was a dream come true. I spent the entire time hiding behind something or someone so I could stare at her, so I could record her every gesture and movement in my head. My brain turned into a video camera so that my heart could rewatch the best movie ever made on the face of the earth whenever I wanted to.

I don't know where I found the courage to ask for her number. In fact, I didn't. Silvia gave it to me—they're friends—after the summer break. But I don't think she told her it was me who wanted it. Perhaps that's why she's not replying. Maybe she doesn't know it's me writing. I've listed her as "Red" in my contacts. Red star: sun, ruby, cherry. She could at least answer out of curiosity.

But wasn't I a lion in my previous life? That's why I don't give up. I lurk in the forest, and when the moment is right, I jump out from the trees and seize my prey, cutting off all escape routes by forcing it into a clearing with nothing to hide behind.

That's what I'll do with Beatrice. She'll find herself face-to-face with me and will be forced to choose me.

We're made for each other. I know it. She doesn't. She doesn't know she loves me. Not yet.

I talked to Terminator today. Yes, because when I have important issues to resolve, I know there's no point in speaking to grown-ups about them. They either don't listen or they say, "Don't worry about it. It'll pass." But if I'm telling you about it, maybe it hasn't passed, duh! Or they come out with the classic: "One day you'll understand, one day when you have children you'll understand, one day you'll have a job and you'll understand."

I just hope that day never comes, because everything will weigh you down at once: adulthood, children, work . . . And to me it seems crazy that all those things have to hit you, like some kind of flash of lightning, just so you can understand. Wouldn't it be better to start now, a bit at a time, without waiting for that stupid day? Today. I want to understand today, not *one day*. Today. Now. But no: that day will descend on you and it will be too late, because you, who wanted to be prepared for it, found nobody who could be bothered to give you an answer. You just came across someone who warned you about it, as if it were some kind of prophecy of death and destruction.

Not to speak of teachers. When you try to have a serious conversation with them, they always say, "Not now," which translates as "Never." They're quick to tell you the bad news:

grades, tests, write-ups, homework . . . but they never tell you the good things otherwise. They say, "You're resting on your laurels," which doesn't sound that comfortable. Other than that, there's not much else to talk about with them.

Mom and Dad? No way. The mere thought makes me shudder. They act as if they've never been my age. And anyway, Dad always comes home tired and wants to watch soccer. Mom? I feel awkward with her. I can't be talking to Mom at my age! So, teachers are out, parents are out, and Niko hasn't spoken to me since the match against Fantacalcio. Who does that leave me? Terminator. At least he just listens and says nothing, especially if I give him fried cat-flavored biscuits afterward.

"You see, Terminator, ever since The Dreamer talked to us about dreams, the subject keeps coming back to me, like an annoying itch, but much deeper. What did you want, Terminator? What did you want to be when you grew up? I guess all you can be is a dog: eat like a dog, sleep like a dog, pee like a dog, and die like a dog. Not me. I like big ideas. A great dream. I don't know what it is yet, but I like dreaming and having a dream. Just lying in bed in silence and dreaming my dream. Nothing else. Going through all my dreams and seeing which ones I like. I wonder if I will leave a mark. Only dreams leave a mark."

Terminator tugs on his leash. Even he can't concentrate, and I wonder what he wants. We keep walking.

"Don't interrupt me! I like having dreams. I like it. But how can I find my dream, Terminator? Yours came ready-made, but I'm not a dog. The Dreamer had his granddad with his stories, and that film he wrote about on his blog. Maybe I should go to the movies more often, seeing as I haven't got a granddad, and Grandma smells funny. She has that musty smell that I hate, and it makes me sneeze. Plus I have to shout things at her because she's a bit deaf. Or maybe I should read more books. The Dreamer says that our dreams are hidden in things we come across in real life, things we love: a place, a book, a page, a movie, a painting . . . Dreams are loaned to us by the great creators of beauty.

"That's what The Dreamer says. I don't quite know what it means. But I know I like it. I should try. I need some advice, but without believing it too much, because I'm the kind of guy who keeps his feet on the ground. A life without dreams is like a garden without flowers, but a life full of impossible dreams is like a garden full of fake flowers . . . What do you think, Terminator?"

Terminator replies by peeing on a lamppost. The length of his pee is proportional to the length of my ramblings.

"Thanks, Terminator. You really understand me . . ."

Beatrice must be sick. The flu's going around, but I never seem to get it. I haven't seen her for two days. Days seem emptier without the red shimmer of her hair. They become white like days without sunshine.

I go home with Silvia. I give her a lift on my Batscooter, and she constantly asks me to slow down. Women. We talk at length and I ask her if she has a dream, like The Dreamer. I tell her that Niko has a very clear dream. He says he will follow in his father's footsteps. His father is a dentist. Niko has a ton of money. He's going to study dentistry and then work in his father's surgical office. He says that's his dream. But I don't think that counts as a dream. Because he already knows everything about it. Dreams—if I've understood correctly—need an element of mystery to them: something yet to be discovered. And Niko already knows it all.

I don't have a clear dream yet, but that's the beauty of it. It's so mysterious that I get excited just thinking about it. Silvia has a dream too. She wants to become an artist. Silvia is very good at painting, her favorite hobby. She even gave me one of her paintings. She copies famous works of art. It's a lovely portrait of a woman shielding herself from the sun with a white umbrella. It's a special painting because the woman's clothes and skin are so pale they blend into the sunlight shining on her. It's as if she's made of the light she is protecting herself from. And it is the only case in which white doesn't scare me. Silvia managed to fool the white in this painting. I like it. After at least a dozen near misses, thanks to my brakes that need work, we stop outside Silvia's house.

"But my parents don't want me to. They say it can only be a hobby and certainly not my future. They say it's a hard road to take, only very few manage to succeed, and you risk an impoverished life if you don't have a breakthrough."

Grown-ups exist solely to remind us of fears we don't have. They are the ones with fears. Me, on the other hand, I'm glad Silvia has her dream. When she talks about it, her eyes shine, like The Dreamer's eyes when he explains things. Like the eyes of Alexander the Great, Michelangelo, Dante . . . blood-red eyes, full of life . . . I think Silvia's dream is the right one. I ask her to look into my eyes and tell me when they shine. That way I might discover what my dream is while I'm talking to her about something and maybe am distracted and don't realize it on my own. She agrees.

"When I see your dream shining in your eyes, I'll tell you."

I ask her to paint me another picture. She says she will. Her eyes light up, and I can almost feel her gaze warming my skin. They shine deep blue. That is her dream. I still don't have one, but I can feel it is on its way. How do I know? My dark circles. Yes, I have bags under my eyes to carry dreams in. When I find the right one I will empty the bags, and my eyes will become light and sparkly.

I ride off into the blue of the horizon, and I feel like I am almost flying, without brakes and without dreams.

Beatrice still hasn't come back to school. She doesn't even go to the bus stop in the afternoons. My days are empty.

They are white, like Dante's were when he no longer saw Beatrice.

I have nothing to say because words end when there is no love.

Pages become white. Life's ink has run out.

I finally spoke to The Dreamer.

"How does someone find their dream? And don't tease me, sir."

"Look for it."

"How?"

"Ask the right questions."

"What do you mean?"

"Read, look, be interested . . . and do everything with enthusiasm, passion, and hard work. Pose a question to each of the things that rouse your interest and excite you. Ask each one why it does so. That's where the answer to your dream lies. It's not how you feel that counts, but what you love."

That's what The Dreamer told me. How he comes up with these things, only he knows. I need to discover what's important to me. But the only way of finding that out is by dedicating time and effort to it, and that doesn't convince me . . .

I'll try to follow The Dreamer's method: I should start from what I already know. I care about music. I care about Niko. I care about Beatrice. I care about Silvia. I care about my scooter. I care about the dream I don't know yet. I care about Mom and Dad when they're not annoying. I care about . . . Maybe that's all. Those aren't enough things. I need more. I have to make an effort to find them and pose each one the right question.

I ask myself why I care about Silvia. I tell myself it's because I'm fond of her, I want her dream to come true, and when I'm with her I feel at peace deep down, like when Mom used to hold my hand in the supermarket. Why Niko? I answer that it's because I like being with him. I don't have to explain anything. I don't feel judged. Speaking of which, I need to do something about him. This silence has to end. We have another match soon, and if we're not in step with each other, the Pirates will end up shipwrecked.

Then I ask the question about my music, and the answer is that I feel free with my music. I ask my Batscooter without brakes and get the same answer. I have some pieces of the puzzle: I care about people's affection, I care about freedom. My dream has those ingredients. At least I've found some of them. But it's still not enough.

Why do I care about Beatrice? That's tougher, and I haven't found an answer. There's something mysterious about her. Something more that I can't work out. A mystery as red as the sun that rises and makes the night darker just before dawn. She is my dream, period. That's why it can't be explained. Stuff that keeps me awake. I watch a horror movie. Stuff that keeps me awake. Sleepless night to the nth degree.

This was the only Greek homework I enjoyed in school. We had to take a few words from a Greek text, then write in our exercise book their meaning and an Italian derivative word that would help us remember the Greek term. That's how I learned two words really well.

Leukos: white. The Italian word *luce* derives from this: light.

Aima: blood. The Italian word *ematoma* derives from this: blood clot.

If you join those two frightening words together, they form an even more terrifying one: *leukemia*. That's what blood cancer is called. A word derived from Greek (all the names of illnesses come from Greek), and it means "white blood."

I knew that white was a rip-off. How can blood be white?

Blood is red, period.

And tears are salty, period.

Silvia told me in tears:

"Beatrice has leukemia."

And her tears became mine.

That's why she hasn't been coming to school. That's why she disappeared. Like Argentieri's husband. Worse, in fact: blood cancer. Leukemia. Maybe it can be cured though. Without Beatrice, I'm finished. My blood will turn white too.

That stuff about dreams is pure garbage. I knew it. I've always known it. Because then pain comes, and nothing makes sense anymore. Because you build, build, build, and then suddenly someone or something tears everything down. So what's the point? Beatrice was in my dream, and Beatrice was the mysterious part of the dream. The key that opened the door. And now this thing arrives that wants to take her away from me. If she disappears, my dream disappears. And night remains in the darkest of darkness because there will be no dawn.

Why the hell does an illness like this exist, one that turns blood white? Dreamer, you're a liar of the worst kind—one of those who actually believe the lies they tell! Tomorrow I'll slit the tires of your loser bicycle. Now I'm hungry. Text message: "Niko, I need to see you."

Afternoon at McDonald's: the saddest thing in the galaxy. It smells of Big Macs and of the loser kids from middle school. But who cares? This'll do. I've never mentioned Beatrice to Niko. Beatrice has always been my secret. A Caribbean island with crystal-clear water, where I can seek refuge alone. With Niko I talk about hot babes, about chicks . . . Beatrice isn't a chick, and even if she's hot, she doesn't belong in that category. She isn't part of the "X-ray group"—the ones you size up to check out what they've got. No, you don't touch Beatrice, not even with words. I don't talk about Beatrice this time either, and I keep all my anger and pain inside. Niko arrives and sits next to me, annoyed.

"What is it?"

"Come on, let's stop acting like idiots. Pirates don't squabble like girls."

Just what Niko was hoping for. He smiles and his eyes seem to melt. He gives me a poke.

"We really are a pair of jerks."

"Speak for yourself."

We laugh. As we guzzle two giant Cokes and Niko modulates a few burps, we talk. We talk some more. We pick up exactly where we had left off. Like only true friends know how to do.

"We need to play some music. We haven't let loose in a while."

"Yeah, and we need to get ready for the next match."

"Who are we playing?"

"Those slow coaches from 3A."

"The X-Men?"

"Yes."

"Easy."

"Niko?"

He stares at me.

"Are you scared of death?"

"What the hell does death have to do with sitting in a McDonald's with a giant Coke in front of you? You're nuts, Leo. I think it's your hair. You should cut it. It's keeping the oxygen from reaching your brain."

I burst out laughing, but in truth I've turned to ice.

"What have I told you a thousand times?"

I imitate his metallic voice: "You mustn't think about white!"

"Come on. Let's go and pick up girls in town—"

"No, I need to get home . . . and to study . . ."

Niko laughs.

I pretend to laugh.

"See you tomorrow. We'll crush them!"

It's not easy being weak.

Silvia tells me that Beatrice is in the hospital. Only Silvia has the right to tell me certain things. Beatrice needs blood. Blood transfusions of her same type. The white blood must be fought in the hopes that new, clean, red blood forms. Fighting the white blood can save her. I don't know what her blood type is, but I know I have so much red blood in my body that I would give it all to her to see hers turn as red as her hair. Blood-red hair.

I fly on my Batscooter without saying anything to anyone. Everything has turned white: the road, the sky, people's faces, the front of the hospital. I go in and am overwhelmed by a smell of disinfectant that reminds me of the dentist's office. I look for her room. I don't ask where it is because I have a compass in my heart that always points toward her North: Beatrice. Indeed, on my third attempt, I find it. I peer in and look at her from a distance: she's sleeping. Like a sleeping beauty. There's a lady next to her with red hair. Her mother, maybe. Her eyes are closed too. I don't have the courage to get closer. I'm frightened. I don't even know what to say in these circumstances. Silvia might know, but I can't always call her.

Then I remember about dreams and that Beatrice is my

dream. So I go to the hospital reception desk and tell them I'm there to give my red blood to replace Beatrice's white blood. The nurse on duty looks at me, perplexed.

"Look, we don't have time to waste around here."

I glare at her. "Neither do I."

She realizes I'm being serious.

"How old are you?" she says with a look of distaste.

With a look of distaste: "Sixteen."

She tells me that minors need permission from their parents. That's a good one! You want to give blood for a person who's sick, but you need permission. You want to build a dream, or save one, but you need permission. What a world! They push you to have dreams, then stop you in your tracks. They're all envious. So they claim you need permission to dream, and in order to *not* need permission, you must be an adult. So I go back home. I feel like I am floating on a sea of white, with no harbor, with no haven. I've accomplished nothing. I didn't talk to Beatrice, and I didn't give her my blood. I'll call Silvia, or this will end badly.

"How are you?" I ask.

"So-so. You?"

"Bad. They didn't let me give blood for Beatrice!"

"How come?"

"If you're a minor you need permission."

"That makes sense. It could be dangerous—"

"Love makes everything possible! You don't need permission!"

"I guess . . . ," Silvia replies, then says nothing.

"What's up? You seem weird today."

She mechanically repeats my second-to-last sentence, as if she weren't listening to me:

"Love makes everything possible . . ."

I can't concentrate on anything. My dream is disintegrating like a sandcastle when the tide comes in and reduces it to a pile of rubble just a few inches high. My dream has become white because Beatrice has cancer. The Dreamer says I must pose the right questions to discover my dream. So let's try with this damned leukemia! Why the hell did you come between my life and Beatrice's? Why are you poisoning the blood of a life that is so full and just beginning? There is no answer to this question. It's the way it is—end of story. And if that's the way it is, there's no point in dreaming. Or at least it's better not to, because it hurts more. It's better to have Niko's kind of dreams, the safe ones, the ones you can buy. I'll go and buy myself some new shoes, a pair of dreams. At least I can wear my dream on my feet and trample it.

I keep my feet firmly on the ground and trample my dream. The Dreamer says that desires have to do with stars: *de più sidera*, which means "stars" in Latin. All bollocks! The only way to see stars is not by desiring, but by hurting yourself.

"Where the heck are you?"

Niko's voice bellows out of my phone and wakes me from my slumber. It takes me a split second to realize it's 5:00 p.m. and that our match against the X-Men is in a half hour.

"I had to clean up my room, or Mom wouldn't let me go anywhere . . ."

Niko doesn't believe me for a second.

"Move it. We need to reclaim first place in the tournament."

He ends the call.

For the first time in my life I forgot about a match.

I don't know what's happening to me. I must be sick. I take my temperature, but I'm fine.

I join in the Pirate battle cry that we yell before every match:

"Beach that whale, Pirates!"

We humiliate the X-Men 7 to 2, and I score three goals.

But inside something prevents me from being truly happy about it. I can imagine that whale. It's huge. It's white. And I'm terrified that it will swallow me up.

The Dreamer has come up with another impromptu lesson. They're the best!

He starts reading an extract from a book that impressed him, something he is studying or researching on his own time. He reads it with his eyes shining, like someone who can't help but share his joy with whomever he meets on the street. Like when I say "Beatrice" out loud without realizing it, or when I want to tell everyone that an oral test has gone well, which rarely happens . . .

This time he reads us a story from the book *Decisive Moments in History*, which talks about three sieges and three pillages.

"Rome, Alexandria, and Byzantium. Three cities packed with treasures, beauty, and art. Three cities with libraries full of books that preserved the secrets of centuries of literature and research. Buildings brimming with scrolls and codices covered in those men's dreams, that could have been useful for the dreams of so many others yet to come. But those dreams went up in smoke amid the blazing attacks of the Barbarians, Arabs, and Turks. In one flaming gesture they destroyed floors and floors full of papers containing the secrets of life. They burned the spirit and its wings. They stopped it from flying as it had done for centuries, freeing themselves from the confinement of history. The pages of books burned like those in the marvelous novel by Ray Bradbury, which you should read . . ."

These are The Dreamer's words. I don't know exactly what they mean but they sound good, even though I've never heard of that Bradbury guy.

At the end of his passionate speech The Dreamer asks us, "Why?" None of us is able to answer. He tells us to think about it and then write something down for homework. The Dreamer is nuts. He thinks we are capable of such thoughts. We have to solve much simpler and more concrete problems. Things that are immediate and useful: like where to copy a Greek translation, how to get a date with a cute girl, how to squeeze money out of your parents to top up your cell phone after you've run out of credit in just two days by sending text messages no longer than five or six words each . . . That kind of stuff. We're not used to answering the profound questions The Dreamer poses. We're not ready for those things. We don't even know where to find the answers.

Because the answers to the questions he asks aren't the kind you find on Google. If you type in *Rome, Alexandria, Byzantium, fire, dreams, causes, books*, you get no results. Because there is nothing on the internet that brings together such disjointed words. You need to come up with the connection yourself somehow. That's why it is so difficult.

I don't know if I'll do this assignment. It's really difficult, but there is something mysterious about it because, for the first time, you can't copy the answer from somewhere. You need to find it yourself. Perhaps there is more at stake too. I'll give it a shot. I hate The Dreamer because he always makes me curious.

Ignorance is the most comfortable thing I know, aside from the sofa in my living room.

I try to talk to my mom about the blood I would like to donate to Beatrice, but she doesn't get it. To her it seems like some kind of vampire story, like those that are popular right now. I explain the situation. She says we'll talk about it later, that it seems like a nice idea, but that surely plenty of others will have already thought of it. I insist.

"Talk to your father about it."

The magical phrase for passing the buck since the dawn of time. That's what I'll do. I call Niko and go to see him. I am supposed to do The Dreamer's homework, but I can't think of anything. Maybe music will help. Sometimes in music you find the answers you're looking for, almost without looking for them. And even if you don't find them, at least you find the same feelings you are experiencing. Someone else has felt them. You don't feel alone. Sadness, solitude, rage. Almost all the songs I like talk about these things. Playing them is like tackling those monsters, especially when you can't even give them a name.

But then, when the music is over, those feelings are still there. Sure, perhaps now you can recognize them better, but they haven't been magically swept away. Maybe I should get drunk for them to disappear. Niko says it works. Beatrice is still sick, and before getting drunk I want to give her my blood. I wouldn't want the alcohol to hurt her because she is pure. I need to speak to Dad.

Now.

Dad didn't come home for dinner. When he got back it was so late that I didn't have the courage to ask him anything. It wasn't the right moment. He would have flared up at me, and I couldn't blow my only chance. I am still awake because I'm trying to do my homework for The Dreamer. I've never given a flip about difficult assignments. When I can't do them, I just go to sleep and copy them the next day. I don't know why, but in this case there is something more at stake, something that is pushing me to accept the challenge. As if throwing in the towel means betraying The Dreamer or myself.

I am in front of the computer screen. I type out the title of the assignment: "Why were Rome, Alexandria, and Byzantium burned down by their conquerors? What motivated the pillagers? What made them similar despite being so different?" White. My mind is blank. White like this stupid screen. White like Beatrice's blood. I call Silvia. She doesn't answer. Silvia always leaves her phone on because she wants me to be able to call her anytime I need help. Silvia is my guardian angel. The only difference is that she sleeps at night and sometimes, like now, she doesn't feel her phone vibrate. Guess I need to solve this myself.

It's late. Outside is the black of night and my mind is white. I try to turn into one of those pillagers and ask myself what

I want to achieve by burning those books. I wander through the dusty streets of Rome, Alexandria, and Byzantium, which I later discover became Constantinople and then Istanbul, and in the midst of the shouts and screams of people, I set fire to thousands of books. I put an end to all those paper dreams, turning them into ash. I turn them into white smoke.

That's the answer. To incinerate dreams. To burn dreams is the way to definitively defeat our enemies so they no longer have the strength to get up and start again. To ensure they no longer dream about the beautiful things in their cities, about the lives of others, about the stories of others so laden with freedom and love. To ensure they no longer dream anything. If you don't allow people to dream, you turn them into slaves. And, as a pillager of cities, I now need only slaves in order to reign happily and undisturbed. And so words upon words should no longer exist—only the white ash of ancient dreams. This is the cruelest form of destruction: to steal people's dreams. Camps full of people burned along with their dreams. Nazis were robbers of dreams. When you have no dreams yourself, you steal them from others so that they don't have any either. Envy burns in your heart and that fire devours everything . . .

When I finish writing it's as dark outside as it was before, and it's from the black of night that I have stolen the marks that now fill my white screen. I have discovered something: by studying, by writing. It's the first time this has happened, but I'm not going to make a habit of it . . . And of course the black ink in the printer has run out, so all I can do is print it in color.

Red.

The Dreamer wanders around the desks to check out our research. Apparently everybody did the homework. Anyone who wants to read it out loud is called up, one by one. It's like being immersed in the dust and fire of centuries ago, and yet we are in class. Everybody has written something they are proud of, at least those who have the courage to read aloud. Naturally I'm not one of them. Reading out loud is like singing. The bell rings. We rush to hand our papers in, but The Dreamer doesn't want them. Unbelievable! He'd rather we keep the answers we have found. Keep them for ourselves.

The Dreamer really is nuts. He gives you homework and then doesn't grade it. What kind of teacher doesn't grade your work? He did get everybody to do it though. Even me, in the pitch-black middle of the night. So maybe a grade isn't necessary to make you study. The Dreamer just sits there, even though the class is emptying. He is smiling and his eyes are shining. He trusts us. He thinks we are capable of doing beautiful things. Perhaps he isn't a complete loser.

I won't let the pillagers burn my dreams and turn them into ash. I will not allow anybody to. I risk not getting up again. Because Beatrice needs me and not a groaning heap of rubble. I don't want to forget what I have learned. I don't want to because it is too important, but I have a shoddy memory. I must write everything down, otherwise I'll forget. Maybe the only way to save myself from my memory is to become a writer.

I want to talk to Silvia about it because she is the only one who wouldn't tease me. As if she has read my thoughts, she walks up to me, squeezes my arm, and rests her head on my shoulder.

"What did you want yesterday? I didn't see your missed call until this morning."

"I wanted some help with my research."

Silvia lifts her head and stares at me sadly:

"Of course. What else would you want?"

She lets go of my arm and walks away.

I stare at her as she walks away, feeling that I've missed something—like when Dad says one thing but really means another. Speaking of which, I should talk to Dad before I forget . . .

If there is one thing I'm crazy about, it's doing super-dares with Niko. They're dangerous dares: the kind that give you a rush of adrenaline, that pump your blood so fast you can almost feel it galloping. One of the dares I like best is sudden braking. We race along on our scooters at full speed, braking only at the last second. The winner is the one who stops closest to the car in front of him without hitting it. That's how I wrecked the brakes on my Batscooter. Niko has no chance in this dare, because in the end he always gets scared, whereas I always brake a second *after* my survival instinct tells me to. Just one second makes the difference. This is the secret to winning the dare: do what you have to, but a second later than you should.

When we saw the flaming black Porsche Carrera at the traffic light, we looked at each other and took off on our scooters at full speed. Side by side. The air is the only thing that tries—but fails—to slow us down. The road crunches under our tires as they grip the crumbled pavement. The rear end of the Porsche gets closer and closer, and we're side by side, at full speed.

I glance at Niko, the last time before the final stretch. I can't lose the dare. Only ten yards separate us from the shiny black rear of the Porsche, and Niko brakes. I wait a second, enough time to say, "One." If you don't brake, you're dead. And I don't brake: for a second that feels like a century. Blood whirrs in my ears. My front tire kisses the rear bumper of the Porsche, like a mother with her newborn baby. I turn toward Niko, my windswept hair over my eyes, a rush of adrenaline blurring my vision. I smile like they do in films after winning a duel. Niko owes me the umpteenth ice cream. There is no dare without ice cream.

"How do you do it? My hands pull the brakes even if I don't want them to. The force is stronger than me."

I lick my strawberry-and-vanilla-flavored ice cream.

"Fear is white. Courage is red. When you see white, you have to focus on red and count to one . . ."

Niko looks at me like you'd look at a mentally ill person who thinks they're talking rationally.

"The match is tomorrow. We have to get back into first place. We need to win and hope that Vandal's team ends in a tie."

"Vandal . . . We'll make him pay . . ."

Niko gives me such a hard slap on the shoulder that my nose ends up in my ice cream.

"That's my boy."

He runs off and I chase after him like a clown with a white face and red nose.

Dad and I walk into the hospital where Beatrice is being treated. They check my blood type. It's the same as Beatrice's. I was sure of it, that we have the same blood type, that we live from the same blood. There are things that one just feels. My life is linked to Beatrice's through our blood. They ask me if I take drugs. I say no. I say no because Dad is there and he would blast me and make his favorite threat: "I'll reduce you to the dust of your shadow." You've got to give it to him. It isn't a bad expression.

Afterward, though, when I'm with the nurse, I tell her I smoked a joint a month ago. But only one, just to try it. There was a group of us. I didn't want to be a wimp. And anyway, it was just to try it. The nurse reassures me. Just one doesn't matter. But if I were a regular user I couldn't donate. My blood wouldn't be any good.

End of the chapter on joints. If Beatrice were still to need it, my blood must be perfect, pure, immaculate. As red as my love for her.

They draw quite a bit. It's much darker than I imagined. It's reddish-purple and dense, like my love for Beatrice. The sight of blood coming out of my arm makes me light-headed, and for a moment I feel like fainting—but I resist. Blood, like love, makes your head spin, but it also gives you the strength to overcome your limits. I feel like I've given my life for Beatrice. I'm half dead and as pale as a vampire in reverse: instead of sucking blood to survive, I've given it.

Dad takes me to get breakfast.

"You're as pale as the froth on your cappuccino. I'll get you another croissant. What filling do you want?"

"What a question. Chocolate."

Dad goes to the counter and gets a croissant dripping with Nutella. He sits back down in front of me and smiles, as he only does in the mornings. In the evenings he's too tired to smile after a day's work.

"Does it hurt?" he asks, pointing to the arm where my blood was drawn from.

"It stings a bit, but it's fine."

"Tell me about this girl, what's her name . . . Angelica?"

I've always said that memory is not a strong point in our family.

"Beatrice, Dad. Her name is Beatrice, like Dante's beloved."

"Is she special to you?"

I don't want to talk to him about Beatrice, so I sidestep the question.

"Who's special to you?"

"Mom."

"When did you realize it?"

"The first time I saw her, during a cruise that my parents had given to me as a graduation gift. She had a way of moving, of tilting her head when she smiled, of arranging her long hair when it covered her eyes . . ."

Dad seems to be daydreaming, his gaze lost in a past that passes in front of his eyes like the beginning of a romcom, the kind of movie I can't stand.

"And then?"

"Then I approached her and said, 'Are you also on this ship, miss?' realizing only at the end of my question that it made no sense. In fact, it was pretty ridiculous, given I had just laid eyes on her for the first time."

"What did she do?"

"She smiled and gazed around, pretending she was looking for someone, and said, 'So it seems . . .' And then she laughed."

"Then what happened?"

"Then we talked and talked and talked."

"You did nothing but talk back then."

"Hey, boy, show your father some respect!"

"And what did you talk about?"

"About the stars."

"The stars? And she actually listened to you?"

"Yes, I had a passion for stars. I had bought my first telescope during high school and I could recognize the constellations. So I told her the history of the stars that we saw from the ship's deck. On that cool, clear night, you could see clearly without the use of a telescope. And, unlike other girls, she listened and asked questions."

He stops, as if part one of his romantic movie has ended. So I nudge him.

"And then?"

Dad takes a deep breath and answers in one go, rubbing his cheek to try to hide his face slightly behind his hands.

"Then I gave her a star."

"You did what?"

"I gave her a star. The one that shone brightest in that moonless night: Sirius, the only star that is visible from any inhabited place on earth and that can, on a moonless night, cast the shadow of your body. We promised each other that we would look at it every night, from wherever we were, and would think about each other."

I start laughing. Dad giving Sirius to Mom . . . I pat him on the back.

"How lovey-dovey. And Mom?"

"She smiled."

"And you?"

"I would have given anything for a woman like her to exist in my real life, not just on a cruise."

Dad says nothing more. He doesn't seem to want to add anything else. I get the impression he's about to blush, so he wipes some croissant crumbs from his mouth in order to hide it. Then he looks at me and says:

"I'm proud of you, Leo, for what you've done."

My ears pop, as if I'd been deaf until that moment.

"I think that today you've started becoming a man. You've done something that nobody suggested or decided for you. You chose it."

I say nothing and take advantage of the situation.

"So can I choose another croissant?"

Dad shakes his head resignedly and smiles at me.

"You're just like your father."

It's been centuries since I spent so much time with my dad. "I'm proud of you" is today's motto. For the rest of the day: relax. I need to regain my strength. I'm extremely tired but just as happy.

I didn't see Beatrice again. She's no longer in that hospital. She's gone back home. She's finished her first round of chemotherapy. A kind of antibiotic against cancer. I'm sure it'll do her good. Beatrice is strong: too young and full of beauty to not make it. I'd like to go and see her, but Silvia says that Beatrice doesn't want to see anyone. She is very tired and drained by her illness and doesn't feel like talking. But I'd like to see her. Anyhow, she'll be given my blood now, and it will be like keeping her company from even closer. From inside. United. I hope my blood will do her good.

I feel happy and tired. Such is love.

"What's wrong with you? Can't you run? You're not doing anything right . . ."

I'm exhausted. I shouldn't have played after giving blood. The nurse told me to rest and take things easy. I didn't tell her I was planning to play soccer, but I couldn't miss the match. Now I'm out of breath, and the score is 2–2 against a bunch of terrible second years who are playing their game of the century. I missed an embarrassing number of goal attempts, worse than Vincenzo Iaquinta on one of his worst days.

"You are as pale as Miss Death."

Miss Death is an über-emo girl in our school. A mass of black surrounding a patch of almost translucent white skin. I feel like throwing up and I'm out of breath. I need to rest on the sidelines. My head is spinning . . .

I put my head between my hands and bend over, hoping that some blood will flow back to my brain. My skin is itching and I'm cold.

"I can't do this, Niko."

Niko looks at me with contempt.

The game ends in a tie.

When Curly, Beanpole, and Sponge get back to the locker room, they bad-mouth me.

"Vandal's team lost. We could have overtaken them. Now we're still one point behind. And all because you've turned into a wimp who can't even stick out one match."

"I went to give blood today . . ."

"And you had to go and do that *today*? The day we had a match?"

I don't bother answering.

I leave the changing room and let the wind dry the tears of anger streaming down my face. Whenever you do good in this world, you always pay for it. People know nothing about love. They only think about soccer and don't even ask *why* the hell you decided to give blood . . .

Beatrice has come back to school. She's thinner. Whiter. Her hair is short, its red color duller and more opaque. Her eyes are still green, but more concealed. I'd like to bump into her and tell her I'm here, that I gave blood for her, that I'm thrilled to see her, but then I realize it's better to keep quiet. I limit myself to smiling at her when we cross paths during break. She looks at me for a moment as if she recognizes me and smiles back. Her smile is not red like it usually is. It's whiter. But she's the heart of my dream. My dream is red, and I must turn that white back to the purple-red I saw coming out of my arm. I have no more doubts. That smile contains the meaning of everything I am searching for.

I won't let you go, Beatrice. I won't let that white cancer take you away. At the cost of putting myself in your place. I won't let it happen, because you are far more needed on this earth than I am. I want you to know that. For this reason I'm going to write you a letter, to tell you that I'm here for you and if you need anything, you can ask me anytime. I will go home today and write the letter. It has to be the most beautiful and reddest thing I've ever done in my life. It has to be perfect.

It's strange how dreams can give you a kick, like a blood transfusion. As if the blood of a superhero is entering your veins.

I've never written a letter and I can't even find one on the internet. Things on the internet are always old. There can't be a letter from Leo to Beatrice. I have to be the first to write it. But I like this because I'll write something that nobody has ever written. I'm excited. I'll get pen and paper now and start writing.

First problem: paper without lines. I'll write it on the computer. But I give up as soon as I start because it's as white as ice. I go back to my sheet of paper and start writing again, but my lines come out all crooked, the words falling into a ditch. It's terrible: all because of the total whiteness. I can't send her an unreadable letter. What can I do?

I get an idea. I print a white page with thick black lines, a bit like Dad's pajamas. I position it under the plain white sheet and use the lines as a hidden guide. Great idea! To defeat the white that makes you write crookedly, you need hidden black lines that are thick and strong. Now it's just a question of filling those lines. That is the hardest part.

Dear Beatrice,

How are you? I saw you back at school the other day. I smiled at you and you smiled back. I don't know if you remember. Well, that was me. The one with wild hair: Leo.

I'm writing because I want to be here for you right now. I'm not quite sure what one is supposed to say in certain circumstances. Whether I have to pretend that I don't know you're sick, whether I have to pretend that I didn't give blood for you, whether I have to pretend that I don't like you . . . Basically, I can't pretend. So there you have it, I've already said it all: you're sick, I gave blood for you, I like you. Now I can speak more freely because I've said the important things. The things that need to be said—because if you don't, you're pretending, and if you pretend, you feel bad. Instead, I want to be honest with you, because you are part of a dream. Just as Mr. Dreamer tells us. I mean, Dreamer isn't his last name, but he's the one who is replacing Mrs. Argentieri, and as he always goes on about dreams, we've nicknamed him The Dreamer. I'm searching for my dream. The trick is to ask the right questions. Ask the right questions to the things and to people we care about, and listen to what our hearts say in return. And you—do you have a dream? Have you ever thought about it?

Sending you a big hug and hope to hear from you soon.

Leo, from 3D

I don't have Beatrice's address. I don't even have an envelope, which is probably for the best. I wouldn't even know how to write the address, where to put the stamp, and all the rest. I'm too embarrassed to ask Mom. So I go out. Get my scooter. Buy an envelope. Put the letter inside it. I write "To Beatrice" on the front of it in giant letters, then I go to Silvia's place to ask her for the address so I can put the envelope in Beatrice's mailbox.

My Batscooter is a flying carpet of happiness, hurtling toward its destination. I can't possibly entrust the letter of my life to the Italian postal service. And so I fly off toward the blue, like the messenger delivering a million-dollar inheritance. My heart beats to the rhythm of my scooter's spinning wheels. I laugh, I sing, and I hear nothing. Not even a horn beeping loudly on my right to remind me that I should have fixed my brakes. And this isn't a last-minute-brake dare. I didn't even have time to be scared this time, to count to one, or to brake . . .

Then, white.

When I wake up I'm in a white hospital bed. My mind is white.
I can't remember anything. It feels like my head is detached from the rest of my body. I've probably been kidnapped, sedated, and turned into a superhero. I wonder what powers I have acquired: flight, time travel, invisibility, mind reading . . . I try to time travel but realize I can't budge an inch. It's because there's something rigid around my neck that is keeping my head and chest blocked. For the first time I understand how Terminator must feel when I pull on his leash.

I open my eyes. Mom is by my side. She has red eyes.

"What happened?"

Mom tells me I was hit by a car. At least, that's what those who witnessed the accident said. I don't remember much, and if anything, just something hazy and confused. Anyhow, the fact is I have a cracked vertebra and have to stay in bed without moving for at least ten days. As if that weren't enough, I have a broken wrist, my right one, and it's already in a cast—so no homework. But who caused this near disaster? Mom tells me that whoever crashed into me didn't stop. He fled. A passerby made a note of the license plate, so Dad will deal with it. The important thing now is that I'm okay and will be back on my feet quickly, but I can say goodbye to ski week and to snowboarding for the rest of the year. By the time I get out of here it will practically be Christmas.

I'm overcome by a surge of anger I didn't know I was capable of. A rage so strong I could even take it out on my mother, even though she has nothing to do with it. Now I remember. I was taking the letter to Beatrice. I had just left Silvia's house after writing the address directly on the envelope. Then darkness. Who knows where the letter ended up. It *was* in my pocket. Now I'm wearing pajamas, a neck brace, and a cast . . . Who knows where the letter ended up.

Hell. Once again you try to do something good, and for some reason you end up on the pavement. Who the hell invented bad luck? And what do I have to do with it? How am I to blame? I'll just quit loving and to hell with everyone.

At least I've realized which superhero I've turned into: Loserman.

I've slept for at least a century, judging by the headache I have when I open my eyes and by how the light hurts my pupils. As soon as I manage to focus on who and where I am, I see a pair of eyes as pale as dawn when it struggles to break. They are Silvia's eyes, as blue as a cloudless sky. Silvia is the Blue Fairy and I am Pinocchio. She makes me feel normal, even in my plaster armor. I smile, squinting. Silvia runs to close the curtains so the light doesn't bother me.

"Are you thirsty?"

She asks me even before I've managed to connect my dry mouth to my brain and my brain to my dry mouth so it can formulate the request. She pours me a glass of pineapple juice that she bought especially for me. My favorite. I haven't yet had the chance to say what I want, and Silvia has already satisfied it. If she weren't just a friend, perhaps I could love her.

But love is something else. Love doesn't bring rest. Love is insomnia. Love is to the nth degree. Love is fast. Love is tomorrow. Love is a tsunami.

Love is blood-red.

Niko comes to visit me. At first he keeps staring at the ground.

"Sorry, Leo, about the other day at the match. Just think if you'd died . . . You'd have left me on my own with that bunch of losers. No more Pirates, no more dares, no more music . . . and no more of our tricks."

I smile. I'm happy. Our friendship is restored. After the match we had barely spoken to each other. Neither of us felt like apologizing. It was up to him. I was hurt, and that's it.

"How long will you be in limbo?"

"Around a month in a cast. Thankfully it's a small fracture . . ."

"Great, so you'll only miss one match. Let's hope we manage without you."

"Get Twiggy to play. Even if he doesn't have such good feet, he knows how to act on the field. You'll need to do some extra work with him. Anyhow, the next match isn't a hard one."

"But it's no fun without you, Pirate."

I smile. "You'll see. I'll get better quickly and we'll go and win that trophy. Nobody can stop the Pirates, Niko. Nobody . . . Besides, we still have a score to settle with Vandal."

Niko stands up in Italian national anthem mode. With his

hand on his heart, he sings out loud, and I follow suit. We sing at the top of our lungs. When the nurse comes in to see what's going on, we burst out laughing.

"If you don't behave, I'll give the pair of you a general anesthetic! And you—can't you behave even in your condition?"

Niko looks at her, suddenly serious and enraptured.

"Will you marry me?"

The nurse, won over, starts laughing.

Niko turns toward me with a sigh.

"She said yes . . ."

The rest of the class comes to visit me. I'm happy. I wonder why to be the center of attention you have to reduce yourself to this state. Sometimes in life you feel like doing something so disconcerting that others can no longer ignore you: You want to be the center of attention. Especially in moments when you feel alone and want to spit your solitude into the face of others. You imagine throwing yourself out a window so that all those jerks understand what you're feeling and what it means to be left alone. In any case, suffering and having bad luck seem to be the best ways to make the world look after you and love you.

They brought me my favorite comics. Silvia painted a picture for me. It's small. There's a boat in the middle of the sea, its bow pointing toward the blue horizon where the sea and the sky meet. It's as if she painted it from the boat. I've hung it in front of me to keep me company when I'm left alone in this hospital room. It's a two-person room, but for now I'm on my own. Thank goodness. I'd be really embarrassed to pee in a urinal bottle in front of somebody else, perhaps even with the nurse holding it for me . . . For a moment I envy Terminator, who has no qualms about peeing in front of hordes of dogs and dog-walkers. Dogs can't even blush.

Niko brought me a CD so I can listen to it and then we can play something from it when I'm better. My other classmates also brought me things. It's nice to be the center of attention, even if the price to pay is a few broken bones.

It's nice to let people love you . . .

I've had a roommate for a few days. A huge man. Immense. An urban elephant. He has two broken vertebrae. He needs to remain immobile and do everything in bed, even using the toilet. I hate his smell. He stares constantly at the ceiling or the TV, which is basically on the ceiling. Occasionally we speak. He's friendly. He's in a bad way, yet he's relaxed. Sometimes he flares into a rage, when he is in pain or can't sleep. He has a wife who looks after him. His daughter and son come to visit him a lot.

When you're sick it's nice to have family around. How can you manage if you don't have a family, a wife, some kids? Who takes care of you when you're sick? Thanks to The Elephant, I've seen what having a family means. Not that I don't have one. But I can see what I couldn't see before. Because until you experience things yourself, you don't really understand or notice them. Otherwise your parents just seem like a pair of professional ball-breakers who are there to forbid you from doing the things you want to do.

Whereas The Elephant, his wife, and their children have shown this to me clearly: when I grow up, I want a family that is as close as theirs. Because even if you're sick you can feel at peace, and that is the point of a well-spent life: having somebody who loves you even when you're feeling bad. Someone who can stand your smell. Only those who love your smell love you truly. It gives you strength, it gives you peace of mind. And this seems like a good way to hold back the suffering that happens in life.

I have to remember this. I absolutely *must* remember this because it needs to be part of my dream for when I grow up. With Beatrice. I already love her smell. The irresistible scent of dreams, of life, of love.

The Dreamer walks in. I can't believe it. A teacher visiting a student in hospital. Well, a substitute teacher, actually. I feel like a king who is touching the sky with his finger, or something like that. The Dreamer sits next to the bed and tells me about school. The oral exams, homework, and something about the program. The term is drawing to a close, and Christmas holidays start soon. Silver tinsel has appeared on the blackboard, and BeardFace—the janitor with a beard so long and thick you could hang Christmas lights and ornaments on it—has put up his scraggly tree. I can visualize it, and I'm sorry not to be there for one of those rare moments when school becomes fun.

The Dreamer tells me that he also broke his arm playing soccer when he was my age. He shows me the scar left over from the operation. Luckily I haven't needed surgery, and I wasn't conscious when they put my bone back into place. You're spared so much pain by sleeping. The problem is waking up.

Anyway, The Dreamer is really good fun because he tells stories just like anyone else would. I mean, he's normal. He has a life just like mine. He even tells me a joke that isn't actually funny, but I pretend it is so he doesn't feel bad. He asks me how my dream is coming along, and I tell him where I am with it. And I tell him that everything went to pieces with the accident, and anyway, I don't know if I want to pursue it, because every time I put effort into it, something bad happens. First Beatrice, now me. The Dreamer smiles and tells me this is part of true dreams.

"True dreams are built amid obstacles. Otherwise they don't turn into projects; they just remain dreams. The difference between a dream and a project is precisely this: the blows. Dreams don't come ready-made. They reveal themselves bit by bit, perhaps in a different way from that in which we first dreamed them . . ."

The Dreamer is saying I'm lucky to be in bed with a broken back! I don't believe him and I say so.

"I had no doubt."

We laugh. But he explains to me that if I'm in this bed, it's because I was doing something special. I was accomplishing my dream by delivering the letter. And if a dream encounters so many obstacles, that means it's the right one. His eyes are shining. When I say goodbye I get muddled up and call him Dreamer. He laughs and adds that he knows that's what I call him. He leaves and I bite my lip because The Dreamer is so easygoing, even about nicknames. Whoever said that to have authority you have to be unpleasant?

My teacher's visit has put me in a good mood. I want to get out of here, have dinner with Mom and Dad, take Terminator for a pee, play music with Niko, study with Silvia, kiss Beatrice . . . But actually, deep down, The Dreamer also ticks me off a bit because—and I hate to admit it—I want to be like that loser history and philosophy substitute teacher.

Mom found the letter. It's got blood and dirt on it. It was in the pocket of my jeans. She threw the jeans away because they were ripped. But before throwing them away, she checked the pockets. Two euros. A rubber band. A Bart Simpson sticker. Gum. A letter. My blood is on that letter. Now coagulated and dried. And it frames Beatrice's name. It's the second time I've given blood for her. And it makes me happy, just like the first time. I read the letter again. It's a good letter, even if some of the words are blurred, smudged with blood. I have to find a way to get it to her. At the cost of having to drag myself out of this bed!

Gandalf came to see me too. I wasn't expecting it. He has twenty thousand classes, at least eight million students, his own parish, and a hundred or so years to drag around every day in that transparent body of his that resembles the Holy Spirit he believes in . . . Yet he still comes to see me. Not that I mind. Really, I'm touched. I wasn't expecting it. He asks me to tell him what happened. I tell him everything, even about the letter. I feel at ease. I don't tell him everything about Beatrice though. I keep that vague. He tells me I am one of God's favorite sons. I tell him I don't want to hear about God because if he existed he wouldn't have let Beatrice get sick.

"If he is omnipotent and omni-everything, why did he do this to me? Why did he want to make me and others suffer when we've done nothing wrong? God's favorite, my foot. I really don't get God. What kind of God are you if you let bad things exist?"

Gandalf tells me that I'm right. What does he mean, I'm right? I provoke him and he says I'm right? I mean . . . surely priests should at least try to defend their position. Gandalf insists that even Jesus, who was the Son of God, felt abandoned by his father and screamed this to him at the time of his death.

"If God treated his own son that way, he will treat all his favorites the same way."

What kind of reasoning is that? But I have no counter-argument because—says Gandalf—this is what the Gospels say:

"If someone wanted to invent a strong God, he could easily do so. He wouldn't imagine a weak God who even feels abandoned by his father at his moment of death."

Gandalf sees blood on the letter that I keep near me on the bedside table. He tells me it reminds him of the crucifix: a letter written to mankind, signed with the blood of God, who saves us all with that blood. I have to stop Gandalf or he'll preach a ten-thousand-hour sermon, and I don't think there's a need for that now. In any case, he's given me food for thought, and I like the thing about the blood. Like I did with Beatrice. Maybe it's the only true thing in that whole discussion about Christ: Love is giving blood. Love is blood-red.

"Leo, there is no good answer to why we suffer. But ever since Christ died on the cross for us, there is a sense. There is meaning . . ."

I give him an affectionate hug, as best as I can. He's already gone when I realize he left his crucifix on the letter for Beatrice. On the back of the T-shaped piece of wood are the words: "To give one's life for one's friends, there is no greater love than that." Not a bad phrase. I want to remember it. I put the crucifix in the envelope. When I go back to school I should return it to Gandalf. Besides, I'm embarrassed to be seen with a crucifix. It brings bad luck.

I am bored with being stuck in bed. Bored to death. The days never end. I'm uncomfortable and my arm itches so much sometimes I'd like to rip the cast off. Minutes never pass. The only way to fill them up is not to think. The TV is on all the time, which is the best form of distraction. Because if I focus on my body I feel pain, and if I focus on my thoughts I feel even more pain. Why has pain decided to become my best friend?

As The Dreamer says, pain is necessary for dreams to come true, so I put up with it, though I'd gladly do without. There must be an easier way to achieve things, possibly without making an effort. I even get tired watching TV. I don't know why, given that I am stuck in bed. But it's a fact. TV wears me out. It's all the same: a general anesthetic. Half the stories on TV are about people's secrets, and the other half are about what they do when their secrets are found out. I have a secret, but I wouldn't go announcing it on TV.

My secret is Beatrice.

Silvia came to see me. She brought me a book. It's a book of short stories.

"To pass the time."

Silvia is like the undertow of the sea. Even if you can't hear it, it's always there. If you listen to it, it cradles you. If I loved her I would marry her in a flash, but love isn't an undertow. Love is a tempest. I ask her about Beatrice. She tells me that she is back in the hospital for her second round of chemotherapy.

"She's here, in the same hospital as you."

I can't believe it. I am sleeping under the same roof as Beatrice and I didn't even know it. This sends me into hyperkinetic rapture. I don't say too much about this to Silvia because it is such a beautiful thought that I want to savor it alone. I want to get back to this thought later, and I need to do something about it. Actually, I'll do it immediately.

"Why don't you take my letter to her?" I ask Silvia.

She says that perhaps it's best not to and lowers her eyes, almost sad. Maybe she's right. Beatrice sleeps a lot during chemo. It wears her out. And she vomits frequently. Silvia hasn't got the courage to go there and give her a letter from someone else. Maybe it's not the right time. I think Silvia is right.

We talk about school. Erika-with-a-*k* is going out with Luca.

They seem inseparable. The weird thing is that Erika-with-a-*k*, who is usually a good student, has already come to class twice unprepared. The day before she had been with Luca. Luca has never studied much and spends entire afternoons in town with Erika-with-a-*k*. They are constantly hanging out and smooching. Erika-with-a-*k* says she's realized that studying isn't important after all. Now that she has love, she's seeing everything else from a different perspective. Because there is nothing like love to make you feel good. Erika-with-a-*k* is right. I agree with her. I tell Silvia that happiness is having a heart full of love. Silvia agrees with me, but she says it's weird that people should change personalities when they fall in love. If Erika has always studied, why stop now that she's in love? She seems to have become any old Erica-without-a-*k*, as if she weren't herself.

Why does Silvia always have to nitpick issues that seem so clear to me? She's even made me doubt the untouchable conviction of being in love. I ask her if she's ever been in love. Silvia nods and stares at her fingertips.

"With who?"

"It's a secret. Maybe one day I'll tell you about it."

"Okay, Silvia, I respect your privacy, but you know you can always count on me to keep any secret."

Silvia smiles hesitantly and then tells me about Mrs. Nicolosi. Nicolosi is our PE teacher. A woman in her fifties who must have been beautiful when she was younger but who isn't anymore. She does everything to appear young, but she looks ridiculous. But nobody has the courage to tell her. She's not like Mrs. Carnevale. Mrs. Carnevale is our biology teacher. And even though she's fifty, she is still a beautiful woman, a beautiful fifty-year-old. Whereas Nicolosi dresses like a twenty-year-old and therefore looks ridiculous. Anyhow, Silvia told me that Nicolosi came to school in a miniskirt and that the guys went crazy.

"Oh no! And I missed it . . ."

Silvia stops short.

"You pig!"

"No, I'm a lion!"

The point is, the guys took photos of her with their phones.

"Don't you like to be looked at?"

Silvia hesitates a moment.

"Yes, very much . . . but I don't want to force anyone to look at me, and a woman knows how to force you. Others prefer waiting for someone who's there just for them and want to be discovered slowly, like one does with a dream."

That's something else I have to think about. Dreams are like stars: you only see them shining when artificial lights are turned off, yet they were there all along. You just couldn't see them because of the brightness of all the other lights. Silvia forces me to think. She does it on purpose. And I fall asleep almost immediately. I wasn't built for pondering at length. I fall asleep with the regret of what I am missing at school. Even though, just before I plunge into darkness, it crosses my mind that I am not actually missing out on anything that's important for living . . .

It's official: school is useless. If I ever become the secretary of education, the first thing I'll do is close down schools.

When I wake up, the first thing that comes to mind is that Beatrice is in the same hospital as me—and I suck on that thought like a mint. It makes me forget the pain, the discomfort, the television. When the most beautiful person you know is near you, everything changes—even the bad things. Initially the bad things don't make sense. Then they do make sense. I must think of a plan. I want to see her, at least. I can get out of bed now. My arm is in a sling and my neck is stiff because of the brace, but I no longer need to stay immobile according to the X-rays.

I make up my mind. I get out of bed. I'm not exactly a marvel of beauty in this state, and I can't even take off my pajamas. But hey, in a hospital you get used to seeing people in pajamas. In fact, it's incredible how quickly you can accept being in your pajamas in front of someone you don't know. That's how things are in the hospital. Maybe it's because we're all as ridiculous as the next person in the face of pain and suffering—so much the same that pajamas are the right uniform to cancel out the differences. Besides, I have a very nice pair of Dad's pajamas. Mom brought them to me because they're bigger and fit over my cast. Also, they smell like Dad, which makes me feel at home.

Looking classy, I venture along the corridors of the women's wing. I don't have the courage to ask the nurses directly about Beatrice, so I wander around as if I'm taking a walk. I peer into the rooms in the oncology department. Silvia told me that's what they call the cancer section. I don't know exactly, but the *onco* bit must be something from Greek that has to do with cancer, because the *-ology* part of the word always has another Greek term attached to it. I should look it up in the Rocci Dictionary when I get home. Rocci is manna for eye specialists! I don't miss it at all. I peer into more rooms. Just like in my wing, most of the patients are elderly. Old. I feel like a kind of mascot. The Elephant is seventy-five . . . The hospital is a gallery of white-haired old people. Young people are in the hospital because of bad luck. Old people are there because they're old.

But if you see a head with a few wisps of red hair resting on a white pillow, like a rose set down on snow or the sun in the Milky Way, that is Beatrice sleeping. Yes, it's Beatrice sleeping. I go in. Her roommate is an old lady so full of wrinkles that they seem to have been etched onto her. She smiles like a crumpled piece of aluminum foil.

"She's very tired."

I smile back. I walk awkwardly toward Beatrice's bed like an Egyptian mummy. I get scared. She has a drip hanging over her with a tube that ends directly in her wrist. It goes into her veins, and the needle that pierces Beatrice's skin allows me a glimpse of her red blood. My blood runs in those veins too. My super red blood cells are devouring her white ones and turning them red. I feel Beatrice's pain weighing me down, and I wish it were my pain and that she were well. I have to be in the hospital anyway.

Beatrice is sleeping. She's different from how I remember her. She's defenseless. She's pale, a strange blue color encircling her eyes, and I know it isn't makeup. She's sleeping. Her arms, flopped at her sides, are concealed by fine, pale-blue pajamas. Her hands are thin and delicate. I have never seen her from so near. She looks like a fairy. She's alone. She's sleeping. I stay there watching her for at least half an hour. She continues sleeping. We say nothing, but it's not necessary. I stare at her face to remember her every feature. She has a small dimple on her right cheek that makes her appear to be smiling even while sleeping. She doesn't make a sound. You can't hear her breathing. She's silent. But as radiant as ever, like a star in the night. Then a nurse comes in to check on her and asks me to leave the room. I get up somewhat awkwardly in my fancy pajamas.

"Do you know her, Mr. Stylish?" asks the nurse, who wobbles about like Spam because of the joke she's just made. I say nothing for a second and then reply with a beaming smile:

"Yes, she's my girlfriend. I had to break an arm just to be near her."

The Spam nurse holds back something more than a smile, something I can't define. Before leaving, I stroke Beatrice's face. I don't wake her though. I want her to find my caress there on her cheek when she wakes up.

Get better, Beatrice. I have a dream. And I need to take you there with me.

I didn't leave Beatrice the letter. I forgot about it, all because of the Spam nurse who distracted me. But maybe it wasn't the right moment. I open the letter to read it again. As if I'm reading it to her out loud. Gandalf's crucifix falls on the floor. It was in the envelope. It wedges itself in the hardest spot to reach, like only things you really need know how to do. My good arm nearly falls off trying to retrieve it. I clutch it in my hand. Fuming. I look at it. The figure is also sleeping. He has the same look that Beatrice has when she sleeps. And I realize that he too understands what Beatrice is going through because he seems to have gone through it.

God, why do good people, supposing that you exist, have to suffer? Of course you won't answer. I don't know if you're there. But if you are and if you make miracles happen, make one happen for me: help Beatrice get better. If you do, I'll start believing in you. What do you say?

I spent the whole day sitting in bed, looking at Beatrice's sleeping face through the microscope of my memory. I snuggled into the dimple on her right cheek and remained there for hours, like a newborn in a cradle, or like when I colored in those unbearable black-and-white coloring books as a child. The world appeared better from there. I felt as if I could listen to the silence without being afraid of it, as if I could touch the darkness. It was as if my withered senses were stretching out after a long sleep. Hours passed in this way, without me realizing it. But not in the same way as watching TV for hours. Because I'm not tired now. I could start all over again.

It's already evening. It's dark outside. I want to protect Beatrice from the night. I get out of bed and head toward her room. I no longer notice the smell of the hospital, but now I can only smell the odor of sick people and I'm less scared of it. I turn back. I can't go empty-handed. I go into a room where I see some flowers in a vase. Two ladies are watching TV. It must be one of those ultra-boring films on channel 4. But they seem to have fallen into a channel 4 hypnotic silence. Old people. I walk up to the vase. I take a daisy. A white one. One of the two ladies turns toward me. I smile.

"It's for a friend."

Her face, which seems to have emerged from a prehistoric cave, gives me a nod. It makes her wrinkles deepen into rivers.

"Good night."

"Good night."

She says it sweetly, relaxing the rivers of her wrinkles into a sea of peace. I leave cheerfully with my flower in hand. This daisy is beautiful. Simple, exactly as a daisy should be. It's as if the seed was planted by someone for this very moment. That gardener didn't know it, but he was doing it for me. His work had meaning for this time and place. In a hospital corridor, in the white silence of night, I am taking a daisy to Beatrice, in room 234 of the oncology department. When I walk into the room, it is in semidarkness. I can only make out the silhouettes of Beatrice and the wrinkled lady. They are already sleeping. They are so alike in the dim light! Both are worn out by their illnesses. They are so similar, yet so different. It isn't fair that a young person becomes old so quickly. Beatrice sleeps. Under the brown hospital blanket I can just make out her profile, which seems to embody all the most beautiful profiles I know. I walk up to her and leave my daisy next to her, on the bedside table. I whisper a song, without shame, without blushing.

"Good night, good night, little flower; good night between the stars and this room. To dream of you, I need you to be close to me, and close still isn't enough."

I walk away in silence. I've done what I had to do: my first-ever serenade. In my pajamas, but I did it.

I go back to bed and can't fall asleep. When I look at Beatrice a brick lodges in my stomach. It's different from the feeling you get when you see a girl who blows you away. There are girls who make your head spin because of their beauty. Beatrice planted a brick in my stomach, a weight I have to bear, a gentle weight . . . which must be the sign of true love. Not just the love that makes you giddy like vertigo, but the love that pulls you to the ground like gravity. That's how I fall asleep with the light on, looking at the painting Silvia gave me. I imagine myself at the helm of that boat with Beatrice by my side, sailing to the island where all our dreams become reality. A daisy nestled in her red hair that blazes in the sun, as if it were made from the sea's surface.

As Aldo, Giovanni, and Giacomo say in one of their movies, "Ask me if I am happy. I am, at least, in my dreams."

I finally get to go home. Christmas is tomorrow and I am being discharged. Great . . . The only present that is wrapped so far is my arm—with plaster! But first I need to leave Beatrice my letter, so that once she gets out of the hospital too, we can see each other. Everything will sort itself out and we will live happily ever after. I'm waiting for the help of nighttime, when the hospital is filled with indiscriminate snoring that spills out of the rooms like the grunts of wild boars. The smell of illness seems to dwindle during sleeping hours, like pain does. I have my letter, in a new envelope I got Silvia to buy for me. It's sealed. I stealthily make my way to Beatrice's room. With every step I feel my soul dilate, and my heart becomes a home that Beatrice has already started to decorate—moving objects, feelings, dreams, projects, as she sees fit. I repeat the words in my letter from memory, as if they are detaching themselves from the paper and taking on a life of their own.

The door of the room is closed. I open it as gently as I can. I walk up to Beatrice's bed almost without breathing so I can hear her every murmur, smell her every scent.

The bed is empty. The sheets are untouched, white, without a single crease.

I sit on the bed. I crumple the letter in my hands until it's crushed. My dream is like those kites I used to build with Dad when I was a kid. Months of preparation, and then they never flew. Only once did a red-and-white kite of ours take flight, but then the wind blew so hard that the string cut into my hand and I had let it fly away because of the pain.

That's how Beatrice is drifting away, carried by the wind. I try to hold her back, but the pain of the thread that binds her to my heart becomes stronger and stronger. I curl up like Terminator does when he sleeps, and the hurt slowly eases as I come into contact with the bed that held Beatrice. Tonight I'll sleep near her, even if she has flown away from here.

"What are you doing here?"

These words interrupt my meandering in an immense white bed with no boundaries. If the Spam nurse hadn't recognized me, I'd be in deep trouble.

"I was looking for Beatrice . . ." I reply with such honesty that it can't help but touch the soft heart shared by all nurses who are fat and capable of loving the smell of sick people.

"She left yesterday."

She says nothing and turns serious.

I pull myself off the bed, weighed down by the nostalgia of someone who has spent the night in Beatrice's arms. I leave the room with my eyes to the ground, dragging my feet. When I walk past the nurse, she ruffles my hair with her soft hand.

"Take care of her. For me too."

I stare at her and feel the warmth of that hand giving me the courage I lack.

"I will."

Later, Mom arrives. She packs all my belongings into a carry-all, and propping me up with her arm even though it's not necessary, she helps me to the car. I pretend to feel worse than I do so she can feel my weight and I can feel her arms around me, making me forget the pain—the heaviest and most invisible thing I know.

My room hasn't changed. Who knows what changes I expected. I no longer sleep under the same roof as Beatrice, nor can I go and see her. My Batscooter has met the end that I could have too. I wouldn't be able to drive it anyway.

It's Christmas and I have to stay indoors with my arm in a sling for another two weeks. "Make the most of your vacation by catching up on your schoolwork," Mom said. Yeah, great vacation, studying twice as much as usual. But twice times zero is zero. I know that at least. When I open my textbooks the hands on my watch seem to stick to the dial and stop moving, trapped in a space-time bubble.

I start floating in this white bubble that carries me up high, far into the clouds, where nobody can hear me, and then into cosmic silence: alone like a balloon that has flown away.

When everything turns white, my heart shrivels up like a lentil, and even if it screams, no one can hear it.

The only one who can save me is Silvia.

Silvia has gone to visit her grandmother by the sea for a few days. Just as well. I can put off the wretched catching-up-on-homework a bit longer. Yet I am bored to death. I feel guilty about time that is just evaporating, but I can't face all those pages I need to catch up on. The Dreamer says that when you get bored it's because you aren't living enough. What kind of a statement is that? It's one of his philosophical manifestos. It's something bigger than me. Maybe that's why I like it. Maybe because it tells the truth: that I'm not living enough. But what does "I'm not living enough" mean? I should ask him.

Niko calls me. Last week we won the match against the Desperados, desperate by name and desperate by nature. We're back on track and the next match is in a month. I wonder if I'll be able to play. This year all my dreams are in the hands of the soccer tournament. I want to lift the trophy for Beatrice and possibly in front of her!

When you get bored it's because your life is boring.

The day comes when you look at yourself in the mirror and you're different from what you were expecting. That's because mirrors are the cruelest form of truth. You don't appear as you really are. You would like your image to correspond with who you are inside, and you wish others could immediately tell by looking at you whether you're a sincere, generous, and friendly person. Instead, you still need words or facts. You have to prove who you are. It would be nice to be able to just show it. Everything would be much simpler.

I'll get myself gym-fit, a piercing, a tattoo of a lion on my bicep (which I don't have) . . . I don't know. Maybe I need to think about it. But these are all signs that tell someone who they're dealing with at a glance.

Erika-with-a-*k* has a nose piercing, and you can tell she's an open kind of person, one you can talk to. Susy has a tattoo beneath her belly button that goes all the way down there. In this case you can tell *exactly* who you're dealing with. In short, I need to make myself more visible so others notice me more. I am fed up with being anonymous.

Beatrice doesn't need to. She has red hair and green eyes. That's enough to tell you how much she can love and how pure she is: as red as the brightest star, as pure as the most Hawaiian sand that exists.

Back at school everybody makes fun of me and calls me C-3PO, the golden droid in *Star Wars*. I still have my arm in a sling, even though in a few days I'll finally get the cast taken off. Apparently not even Giacomo is the biggest loser in the class since I got back, because it turns out I'm even unluckier than he is. To compensate, though, everyone has signed my cast. It is completely covered with my classmates' and friends' signatures. My arm is multicolored. My arm is famous. My arm cares about me, because I now carry about everyone who cares about me. "The Pirates are waiting for their captain! *Niko*." "Your reincarnation will be a monument to bad luck. *Erika*." "Better you than me! *Jack*." "You're still handsome! *Silvia*." There is just one signature missing. Beatrice's. But I don't need it because I carry her name on my heart.

There are names, and then there are names. If you buy yourself something from Fred Perry, Dockers, or Nike, those are brand names you wear. Sooner or later you'll change, throw away, or lose those things . . . Sure, they make you feel good, but they don't last. Then there are other names. Those you carry on your heart. Those names tell you *who* you really are and *for* who you really are. I have Beatrice's name tattooed on my heart. She is my dream and I exist for her.

But Beatrice hasn't been coming to school: a new cycle of chemo. She'll end up flunking the year if this goes on.

When I get home there's a crumpled letter on my desk. A Post-it from Mom says, "This was in the bottom of the carryall with your hospital things." The letter to Beatrice! How could I have forgotten about it? I have to take the letter to her, even if it's the last thing I do, because "It's what you do that defines you, not what you are." Batman is always right.

Compelled by the inexorable passing of days, I'm finally sitting in front of my books. I've decided to catch up on my schoolwork. Actually, Silvia is sitting in front of me because I could never do it on my own. We're in that hair-raising phase of the semester filled with tests and assignments. And I am terribly behind.

Silvia sits there telling me about The Dreamer's lessons (especially his ad hoc ones, my favorites), and she summarizes the syntax of cases and explains a canto of *The Divine Comedy*. The one where Ulysses convinces his mates to face the challenges of the sea in order to seek out, I think, "virtue and knowledge"—I can hear the sharp, metallic voice of my teacher echoing in my ears—but then he tricks them and they all die in the depths of the sea.

As Silvia talks, I drift off. If you think about it, it's always the same old story. People who have a dream, or think they have one, force others to believe in it, but then time and death sweep everything away. Everyone lived in the mirage of that dream. Adrenaline pumps through your veins simply because someone believed it, but it was all an illusion. My dream is an illusion too. Illness wants to take it away from me. Without Beatrice I don't exist.

Silvia looks me straight in the eyes in silence, because she's realized I've drifted off. She strokes me gently and the wind picks up again, making the boat in the painting navigate at full sail toward a harbor I don't know but that I'm certain exists, just like the hand that caressed me. Silvia can do all that with a single caress. How does she do it?

Thank you, Silvia. Thank you, Silvia, for being there. Thank you, Silvia, for being the anchor that keeps me from drifting and for being the sail that allows me to cross the rough sea.

"Thank you, Silvia. You're special."

"So are you."

There are afternoons when my room, which is better than the Euro Disney and Gardaland amusement parks put together, seems like an attic full of old junk. What is the point of life if it's followed by death? And what comes after death scares me. And it scares me even more if after death there is nothing. And God Almighty scares me. Evil and suffering scare me. And Beatrice's illness scares me. Being left alone scares me. And all this whiteness . . .

So I call Niko, but Niko's playing soccer and I can't go. So I call Silvia, but Silvia isn't home. I call her cell phone, but it's switched off. I send her a message: "Call me when you can."

Silvia, could you stroke me like you did last time? I'm scared, Silvia. I'm scared of everything. I'm scared I won't manage to do anything worthwhile in my life. I'm scared that Beatrice might die. I'm scared of having nobody to call on the phone. I'm scared you'll leave me.

I'm in my room and there are only silent things here. Nobody to talk to. My books are silent, and The Dreamer's not here to explain them to me or make me believe I might enjoy them. My comics are silent, despite their colors. My stereo is silent because I don't feel like turning it on. My computer is silent because the screen—deep enough to hold the entire world in it—is only a flat screen when you look at it from the side. And you wonder how it can contain so much world and so much ocean if it's so flat. Everything is silent in my room today. But I don't want to escape. I want to resist. Sadness is flooding into my room in waves today. I try to contain it with a sponge. I'm a joke. I resist a few minutes, then fear assails me and I'm shipwrecked in the middle of an ocean of solitude.

I float in a white desert: a huge, infinite, soundproof white room, in which you can't even make out the corners of the walls. You can't tell which way is up, down, right, or left . . . and I scream, but every sound is stifled. The only things to come out of my mouth are rotten words.

Silvia, call me. I beg you.

When I wake up it's four o'clock and the fear seems more distant, if only because I'm in a complete daze. I've landed on some unknown island. I'm looking for something that can help me survive. The posters in my room are looking at me. Then I see the letter. I have to take the letter to Beatrice. There are two problems. First, the letter is too ruined. It looks like the rough copy of my essays, so I need to rewrite it, but I can't write with my left hand.

The second problem is that I don't know whether Beatrice is at home or in hospital. The first problem has only one solution: Silvia. I dictate the letter, she writes it for me. I know it's not the same, it isn't my handwriting, but Silvia has nice handwriting that's better than mine. As for the second problem . . . the solution is obvious: Silvia!

Am I pushing it? She can call Beatrice to ask her where she is. That way I can take her the letter and maybe even talk to her. Yes, I'll talk to her because I need to talk to her. I need to tell her about my dream, and when she realizes that the dream is necessary, that the dream is our destiny, she'll get better because dreams cure anything bad, any suffering. Dreams give color to all things white.

I head to Silvia's.

Silvia's mother is a lady who appears exactly as she is. I like her. Silvia takes more after her than her father, who is a quiet man and in some ways enigmatic. Silvia's mother has a great gift: she knows how to take genuine interest in me. I can tell by her questions.

"Will you start playing music again soon?"

"I can't wait to . . ."

She asks questions about details. Only those who ask about details have tried to understand what your heart feels. Details. Details: a way of truly loving. I like Silvia's mother. If I could choose my mother, after the one I have, I would choose Silvia's mother.

Silvia's room smells of lavender. That's the name of the crumbled dried flowers in the bowl on the coffee table in the middle of the room. There are no posters on the walls, like there are in my room, but photographs. Photographs of Silvia when she was little, with her parents, with her younger brother, in junior high during a recital, dressed up as the Blue Fairy. I once told her that she is the Blue Fairy and I am Pinocchio. Perhaps Silvia emerged from that book.

Each wall holds one of her paintings: a sailboat suspended in a pale, almost white sky that merges with a milky sea; a forest of spindly trees that she told me are called birches, depicting a scene that made an impression on her during a trip to Sweden; a field of red tulips against a blue, almost purple sky, which instead are taken from a Dutch landscape. I like Silvia's paintings. You can rest in them. You can travel in them.

"I need your help to write something, Silvia."

"On the condition that the day you get better you'll play a song for me . . ."

I wink at her, accompanying the gesture with a click of the tongue against my palate, which is a specialty of mine.

"Which one?"

"My favorite."

"Which is?"

"'Aria' by Nannini."

"I don't know it."

Silvia appears shocked and shows this as only she can: she puts her hands in front of her eyes and shakes her head dramatically.

"You'll have to learn it."

"Can't you make do with Coldplay's 'Talk'?"

"Either that one or nothing," she says, pretending to be offended. Then with smiling eyes she continues:

"What do I have to write? The essay on Dante or the research on cells?"

"A letter . . ."

"A letter? We don't have any homework like that."

"To Beatrice."

Silvia says nothing. She opens a drawer to look for something and her hair covers her face. She takes a while to find paper and a pen. Then she pulls herself up again.

"Sorry . . . Okay, I'm ready . . ."

Silvia writes the letter I dictate. But it doesn't work anymore, and I want to change it. Time has passed, and the words of the first letter are no longer the right ones. Silvia is ready to write. She looks me in the eyes and I try to focus on the words. But they don't come. The words for Beatrice don't come. If I've finished my words for Beatrice, I'm finished too.

Until now the only words I've written freely, given that I don't consider the ones for schoolwork as real words, are precisely the words in my letter to Beatrice. That was—now that I think about it—the first time I wrote something, the first time that words laid bare my soul, black on white. Yes, because the soul is white and to reveal itself it must turn black like ink. And when you see it there, in black, you recognize it, you read it, you look at it, like when you look at yourself in the mirror, and then . . . and then you give it away.

Dear Beatrice,

I am writing this letter to you . . .

My soul starts to emerge, and Silvia turns it into black on white, in her handwriting, and my soul seems more elegant coming from her hands, subtler, gentler, and cleaner . . .

> . . . so that my words may keep you company. I'd love to talk to you in person, but I'm scared of wearing you down and I'm scared of being afraid of seeing you suffer. Therefore I'm writing to you. It's the second letter I've written to you, but the first was left in my pocket. Yes, because I had an accident and ended up in the hospital. So now that I'm better, even if I have my arm in a cast and a neck like a robot's, I've decided to write again. Beatrice, how are you? Are you tired? I guess you are. I gave blood for you. I know that you needed it and I think you'll get better, because my blood will make you better. I'm sure of it. Gandalf claims that donated blood cures people. He says that Christ cured people from sin throughout the ages by giving his blood. But that's a weird story, because in any case that blood has never entered my veins. Even so, I like the idea of blood that cures and I hope that mine will cure you. If you have my blood, you will discover something important. When my blood passes through your heart it will caress it and tell it about my dream. The dream I have. Dreams make people who they are. They make us great.

Silvia stops and asks me if all this business about blood might upset Beatrice, who has probably had enough of needles, hospitals, and blood. Silvia is always right. How can she work out my doubts before me and better than I do? It's almost as if she sees the world through my eyes. So scrap the bit about the blood.

Beatrice, I would do anything for you to get better. I gave blood for you. I hope it helps. Beatrice, I have a dream, and you and I are in that dream. That's why you'll get better, because dreams, if you really believe in them, come true. I know that you are tired and thinner now and perhaps you feel awkward about being seen by others, but I want you to know that for me you're fine the way you are. You're just as beautiful. I'm sure you will get better and, if you want, I'll come and visit soon and we can talk. I have a million things to say and tell you about, even though I think you probably know them all already. In any case, if you're tired and don't feel like talking, we can sit in silence and that's okay too. For me it's enough to be near you.

I stop because my voice breaks, because the image of Beatrice not making it sweeps away all the words in a flash, the image of Beatrice quietly closing her eyes. Not opening them again. The whole world around me becomes dark. The light goes out. The bulb burns out. If Beatrice's eyes don't look at things, those things are lifeless. I've always been afraid of the dark, and I still am, but I don't tell anybody because I'm embarrassed. Silvia looks at me without saying a word. She brings her hand to my eyes and with her finger wipes the tear I've tried to hold back.

"Silvia, I'm still afraid of the dark."

I don't know what made me come out with something so idiotic that it would make even one of those stone statues on Easter Island laugh . . . But Silvia says nothing. She strokes my face. And I stroke hers. Her skin isn't skin: it's Silvia. Then she writes on the letter to Beatrice: "Yours, Leo."

And that "Leo" is written in a way I've never been able to do. And it's written as if it were me. Without Silvia I would be nobody and my soul would remain white. And white is the blood cancer of life.

Silvia dictates the address of the hospital that Beatrice is in. It's different from the first one, because apparently the chemo treatment is different now, longer or something like that. Or perhaps they need to prepare her for surgery.

I'm at home. I take a seriously long shower. I cover every square inch of my body in oodles of deodorant. I look at myself in the mirror for three quarters of an hour, but I'm not satisfied with my appearance. I must be absolutely evident to Beatrice. She must see me and understand who I am. So I try all kinds of combinations of colors and clothes, but I'm unsure about all of them. Something is wrong.

Mom yells at me to get out of the bathroom and stop doing indecent things. Why don't grown-ups understand anything? What do they know about what's going on in your head? They're convinced that the only things in your head are the ones they can't do anymore. Then they complain if you don't ask them for advice. "You're always locked away in your room, I no longer recognize you, you were such a sweet child . . ." Anyway, you already know the answer: "Don't worry, it'll pass." Locked in the bathroom, I try and try again. With my right arm still somewhat inflexible, getting dressed is quite an undertaking, but at least I don't have to die of embarrassment while Mom buttons up my shirt and takes the opportunity to give me a kiss and tell me how handsome I am . . . Maybe a shirt. Maybe a polo with a fleece. Maybe . . . maybe I call Niko.

"Wear a shirt and you'll make a good impression."

Thanks, Niko, you're right. You saved me. Niko always has the right answer, the right recipe, even if he doesn't know the situation. I wonder how he does it. I'd like to be like him and have clear reference points on what to wear in any given situation.

But Niko didn't even ask which girl we were talking about . . .

I'm ready. It's already dark outside, but I carry light within. I have the letter Silvia wrote. I'm hoping to talk directly to Beatrice, and this is also why I've dressed up—because my appearance has to be enough to make her realize how much I love her. Anyway, it'll be enough to leave her the letter.

When I walk into the hospital, a nurse asks me where I'm going and I tell her that I'm going to see a friend.

"What's her name?" she wants to know, with the typical face of a suspicious nurse.

"Beatrice," I reply, looking at her defiantly. The nurse is super skinny—scarecrow-style—and unfriendly. She doesn't know what I'm capable of. I turn my back to her without saying a thing. Then look for Beatrice. And can't find her. No, I really can't find her. After an hour, I'm still wandering around and can't find her.

I've seen all kinds of things. I've visited the museum of suffering, with vomit-green walls and that typical hospital smell of disinfectant. Some people smile when I mistakenly walk into their room. One old man gets angry. He tells me to go to hell, and I tell him to do the same. I walk out of the room and I bump into the scarecrow nurse who glares at me. I lower my gaze.

"Room 405," she says with good-natured satisfaction, crossing her arms as if it were a reprimand.

"How did you know that?" I reply, my eyes lowered.

"She's the only Beatrice in the computer."

I look at her and smile. I blow her a kiss and give her a wink.

"The other way," the nurse shouts at me, shaking her head. "Fourth floor."

I head up the stairs at full speed. I head up and can feel that Beatrice is getting closer. I head up because Beatrice is there and I want to reach her, and every step I climb is a step toward heaven, as it was for Dante in *The Divine Comedy*. The door is closed, or rather, ajar. I open it very slowly.

There is only one bed in the semidarkness of the room, and on that immense, white rectangle there is a tiny, curled-up silhouette. I slowly step closer. It isn't Beatrice. That dim-witted nurse got the wrong room, and who knows where she's sent me. Before leaving, I observe the curled-up figure on the bed. It's a little girl, though at first I thought it was a boy. She has a gaunt, drawn face. Her skin is colorless, an almost translucent paleness. Her arm is purple around the needle that pierces her wrist. But she is sleeping peacefully. She has no hair. She looks like a tiny Martian curled up like a baby in its mother's womb. She seems to smile as she sleeps.

On the bedside table lay a book, a bottle of water, a bracelet made of pale-blue and orange beads, one of those shells that encloses the sound of the sea, and a photo. A photo of that child with her mother's arms around her. On the photo the words: "I am beside you, don't be afraid, my little Beatrice." That child has red hair.

That child is Beatrice.

Silence.

It's midnight. I'm sitting in the place where I sit when the world needs to go back to spinning in the right direction. It's one of those places with a built-in button, the one for going back to the previous song. You push it and the world clicks back into place. You push it and the problem not only disappears, but never existed at all. Basically, one of those places that doesn't exist. That place is a red bench along the river. A place only I know about. And Silvia.

I'm holding my head in my hands, as best I can with my arm in a cast . . . and I haven't stopped crying since I ran away. Yes, because I ran away from my dream. My crushed dream. My hands are clutching the letter for Beatrice that Silvia wrote, drenched by my tears. I rip it into a thousand pieces with my teeth and my good hand. I discard the pieces into the current. There lies my black soul. My written soul.

And now every single fragment of my soul is drowning in the water, each going its own way so no one, no one, will ever be able to gather them up again. I'm drowning in each of those pieces of paper. I'm drowning a million times. Now my soul has gone, the current has carried it away. I want to be alone. In silence. Cell phone off. I want the whole world to suffer because it doesn't know where I've ended up. I want the whole world to feel as alone and abandoned as I do right now. Without Beatrice who is dying, without hair. Without Beatrice, who won't make it. And I didn't even recognize the other half of my dream. I ran away from the girl I wanted to protect for the rest of my life. I am a coward.

I do not exist.

God does not exist.

I wake up suddenly. Happy. It was just a dream. Beatrice is fine. She has red hair. And that is my real dream. God still exists, even if I don't believe in him. It makes no difference anyway. Then I hear somebody's voice saying:

"Leo?"

I shake myself and don't recognize the face I'm seeing. I'm not in my bed. Jack Sparrow isn't looking at me from the wall with his wild eyes, and I'm freezing cold. I'm on my bench and Silvia is standing in front of me with a policeman. This really is a dream. My magic place, Silvia, and a policeman? I stare blankly.

"Are you okay?" Silvia asks, her eyes swollen from lack of sleep or perhaps from crying. I look at her and don't understand.

"No."

The cop speaks into something that I can't make out in the dark.

". . . found him."

Silvia sits down next to me, puts her arm around my shoulders, and, holding me gently, says, "Let's go home."

I look at the black water of the river, in which the car headlights are reflected like trapped fish. My soul is like that right now. Myriads of paper fish that have flown away. Prisoners of the water. They will never come back. And the word *home* is the same as all the others, worse in fact, for who knows what awaits me? I lean my head on Silvia's shoulder and start to cry because of how bad I am.

I don't want to play the guitar. I don't want to eat. I don't want to speak. I'm being punished for what happened. It's only fair, I deserve it. Mom and Dad were desperate when I got back home: bags under their eyes, wretched faces. I had never seen them like that. Because of me. It was four o'clock in the morning. But I got what I wanted. I finally found a way to defend myself from the poisonous scorpion that is reality. To hate is the only way of being more poisonous than the scorpion. Hatred as swift as the fire that devours paper and straw, hatred that burns all that it touches, and the more it touches the more it intensifies. Be bad. Be alone. Be fire. Be iron.

This is the solution. Destroy and resist.

Five hours of lessons. Five hours of war. I tell that dog-fur-wearing Ms. Massaroni to go to hell when she asks me what I was doing with my cell phone. A disciplinary note in my file. I also skip English class and nobody notices. I beat my record in Snake during philosophy, while The Dreamer talks about a guy who claimed that death doesn't exist, because when you're alive there's no death and when you're dead you're dead, so there's no death even then.

To me it seems like total garbage for once. Beatrice was alive before, but now she's dying. Like that poet who wrote that "death is lived by living." I had considered it one of those random claims that poets make, but unfortunately it's true. Beatrice has become unrecognizable, and worse, I didn't recognize her. Death poisons everything about life. Philosophy is useless. T9 doesn't have the word *God*, which proves that God doesn't exist. Snake is the only option left for not thinking about it.

Then The Dreamer opens his usual briefcase from which he can pull out any book, like from Eega Beeva's shorts. And in fact he too—like Eega Beeva—occasionally seems kind of like an alien. Sometimes he doesn't even use any of those books but just leaves them on his desk. He says that to him books are like a piece of his home, and wherever he has them, he feels at home. Books . . . What a load of crap! All those lines full of stories and dreams are not worth the number of the hospital room that Beatrice is in. She's been transformed into a child who is returning to the womb of the earth: swallowed up.

The Dreamer reads out a few letters written by members of the Italian Resistance before being executed, one of his ad hoc lessons. I don't know how he does it, but The Dreamer always has something to say that you can't just switch off. Why doesn't he just leave me in peace? I only listen to him because I can't avoid it, given that you can't close your ears like you can your eyes, but I won't believe a word of it. And when he's finished he can go to hell. This is what he reads:

"'August 4, 1944: Mom and Dad, I die crushed by the grim tempest of hatred, I who wanted to live only for love. God is love and God doesn't die. Love doesn't die . . .'"

The Dreamer pauses.

"Lies!"

I leap up like a fire, burning paper dreams and words of straw. That word hurls itself violently against the teacher's face, like the spiked fist of a night warrior. Everyone turns toward me looking hopeless instead of being gobsmacked by the first declaration of truth ever to be pronounced at school. I'd burn all of them, except Silvia. The Dreamer looks at me too, convinced he hasn't understood.

"Lies!" I repeat, challenging him.

Let's see what you do now, when someone has the courage to say things straight and destroy your castle of literary cards.

For a moment he says nothing. He seems to be searching for something within that he can't find. Then, in a completely calm voice, he asks:

"Who are you to judge this man's life?"

My answer comes out like a barrage. He has thrown fuel on my fire.

"They're all illusions. Life is an empty box that we fill with crap so we can enjoy it, but it takes just one small thing, and *poof* . . ." A silent pause follows the dramatic gesture of my hands mimicking a soap bubble bursting. "You find yourself with nothing. That man was kidding himself, that dying for a cause he regarded as just gave meaning to his life. Good for him. But it's only a sugar coating to make the pill less bitter. The box remains empty."

The Dreamer looks at me again and remains quiet. Then he breaks the silence with a calm and blunt:

"Lies!"

His against mine. Whichever it is, it's still a lie. But it upsets me. I pick up my backpack and walk out, without giving The Dreamer time to say another word. The fire burns and continues to destroy. There's no turning back to offer explanations. They can suspend me, they can even make me repeat the year, I don't care. Nobody can explain what's happening, and if that's the way things stand, why on earth should I make an effort to do anything? I'm alone, and for the first time I am strong. I am fire and I will burn down the whole world. I won't call Niko because he wouldn't understand anything. I won't call Silvia because I no longer need her.

And the image of that child without hair, the pale shadow of Beatrice, makes me want to curse God. I curse repeatedly, over and over again, vehemently. And now I feel better. And I realize that God exists, otherwise I wouldn't feel better. You don't feel any better if you take things out on Father Christmas. But if you take it out on God, you do.

When the fire subsides, I'm drained. Emptied. Around me just dust, ash, blackness. I drift away into the world of the internet: the solution to all problems. You can find Greek homework solutions, essays, films, songs, hot chick calendars. So I type two words in Google: *death* and *God*. Together. Not separate. Together. I get a page about a philosopher called Nietzsche, who said that God died. And we already knew this: on the cross. The next page says the opposite: God rose again, conquering death and freeing mankind from death. This too is unsatisfying, because it's a lie.

Beatrice is dying and nothing can be done about it. This time the internet has got it all wrong. Who cares if Beatrice will rise again? I want her here and now. I want to live with her for every single day of my life and stroke her red hair and her face, look into her eyes and laugh with her and make her laugh and talk, talk, talk without saying anything yet saying everything. Death is a problem that no longer concerns me. Now I just have to deal with life, and since it's so scarce and fragile, I have to make it lavish and strong, full and indestructible. As hard as iron.

Message from Silvia: "Can we study together?" I'm not studying anymore. It's useless. I reply, "No, sorry."

Silvia texts immediately: "Afraid? Afraid of what???" What's she talking about? Silvia's going nuts too. Then I have a thought. I check the message I sent her: "No, afraid." Good old T9. I wrote "afraid" instead of "sorry" without realizing. I hadn't double-checked it and sent it off automatically. "No, afraid." Unfortunately T9 is right. I reply to her message truthfully: "Of everything."

Silence. A silence that drives you mad, a silence that makes you rip your clothes off and scream naked from the balcony that you've had it up to your eyeballs. I am not iron, I am not fire, I am nobody.

Message from Silvia: "Let's meet in the park in a half hour." I reply yes by letting her cell phone ring once. But then I don't go. I let her wait there alone, as alone as I am. I'm a coward and my face is drenched in the most bitter tears I know, the kind where the salt of solitude makes up at least ninety percent and water only ten.

The pain is so dense that you can float on it without needing to swim.

Evening.

Black outside, white inside. I feel guilty. I took it out on the only person who has nothing to do with it and wants to help me. Silence from Silvia. I imagine her alone on the bench, abandoned, her blue gaze fixed on the ground, looking up at every person who approaches. Now I feel even worse. I write her another message: "Sorry. See you tomorrow." White silence. Why do I seek out solitude and then when I am drowning in its whiteness with nothing to cling to, it terrifies me? Why do I want someone to throw me a life buoy, but then do nothing to grab on to it? Maybe I'll understand my capabilities one day, my dreams, but will I ever truly be able to do anything except be a castaway who won't let anybody help him? I'll take Terminator to pee.

Today even he'll do for silence.

I spent the whole night thinking about what to say to Silvia to apologize. In just a few hours my iron shield has melted into cream. I'm worthless.

Whatever. I get to school and look around for Silvia. Her eyes meet mine for just an instant as I'm scouring the crowds: glassy eyes in which I can only see myself and not her. She looks away, as if I'm just anyone. That missed eye contact consigns me to the masses, and I sink back into the white nothingness of a perfect nobody.

I run after Silvia. I grab her arm with more force than I intended. I have never touched her like that, not even as a joke. Silvia frees herself, her face taut with disappointment.

"I fooled myself into thinking I had a friend. Leave me alone. You only know how to ask for help, and you don't care about anyone else."

I don't even have time to open my mouth before she disappears into the distance as if a vortex is pulling her in. I chase after her through the forest of low-rise jeans, bumping into a couple of fifth-year bullies who kick me in the butt.

"Die, idiots."

I see her head turn into the corridor where the bathrooms

are, and without realizing it I follow her into the bathroom full of girls putting on makeup, smoking, and comparing brands of jeans. They look at me dumbfounded as Silvia locks herself in a stall.

"What are you doing in here?" asks a brunette with two black slits for eyes, buried amid a purple smudge of makeup.

"Me? I need to talk to a girl," I retort, as if saying the most normal thing in the world.

"You can wait for her outside. And anyhow, forget it. She's too cute for a loser like you."

They laugh. Those words push me out of the girls' bathroom like the foam on the bare teeth of a rabid dog. I move backward, trying to keep it at bay, and collapse onto a cliff. There is no parachute in the bottomless pit of abandonment.

"What are you doing here?"

Naturally it's the principal who screams at me to follow him to his office. First I run away from Beatrice, then I stand Silvia up, and now I'm being taken for a Peeping Tom. In the space of forty-eight hours I have discovered the existence of shades of black. I have just been through at least three of them, heading toward absolute darkness . . . Pity it's not the end of a tragic film but only the beginning.

My parents, called in for a meeting with the principal because of my bad behavior, are convinced that I'm so incapable of curbing my restless adolescent hormones that I force my way into women's bathrooms. Dad says to me in a whisper, "Consider your bones reduced to the dust of your shadow."

So I get suspended for a day and threatened with a measly conduct grade, which means failing the year. I gloss over the punishment my parents inflict: immediate seizure of my PlayStation until the end of the year and withdrawal of my monthly allowance. It's nothing compared to the fact that the day after my suspension all the girls stare and laugh at me.

"There's the pig!"

"Loser!"

And this is still nothing compared to the insults from the guys.

"Your bathroom is the one without the skirt drawn on the little man. Perhaps we'll add a little line so you remember what you have between your legs!"

Can somebody tell me if there's any way of getting off this carousel of horrors? Or at least if an instruction manual exists showing me how to become invisible?

An entire day staring at the Green Day guitarist's hands on the poster hung on my bedroom door. I start bouncing a tennis ball off it until I make a hole in the paper and maim the guitarist.

I am waiting for two things:

For someone to save me, or for the world to end right now.

The second is easier than the first one.

A phone call: Niko.

"We won, Pirate! The next match determines the final. Vandal is quaking in fear!"

I end the call and hope the bed swallows me up without chewing me first.

The intercom. The intercom buzzes. It's for me. Who can it be at nine in the evening? Silvia. Silvia has surely yielded to the twenty-three messages I sent her today, each time regretting the previous one . . .

"Come down."

It's her.

"Mom, I'm popping downstairs for a minute. It's Silvia."

I go down, but Silvia's not waiting for me. I must have dreamed her voice, convinced as I was that it was her. It's The Dreamer. That's all I need. He's surely come so that he too can say for himself that I'm a spineless good-for-nothing.

"Evening, sir. What have I done?" I ask, staring at a random point on his left shoulder.

He smiles.

"I thought I'd stop by. See if you felt like finishing your speech from the other day."

I knew it. Teachers are teachers until death. They have to lecture you even at your own house.

"Sir, let's forget the other day's discussion . . ."

I really don't know where to start, and I would like all of this to end immediately, like I always do when I don't like something. You switch channels and the scene is gone. Vanished, canceled, finished.

"Let's go and get some ice cream."

He smiles at me. Yes, that's what he said: *ice cream*. Teachers eat ice cream. Yes, teachers eat ice cream and they get their mouths dirty just like everybody else. These are two new discoveries that must never be forgotten, and maybe one day I'll write them down. Speaking of which:

"Your blog is nice. A bit too philosophical at times, but I read it whenever I can."

The teacher thanks me and carries on licking his pistachio and coffee ice cream—usual boring teacher flavors—and he reminds me of Terminator when he licks my tennis shoes.

"So what happened to you the other day?"

I knew he wouldn't let it go. Teachers are like boa constrictors. They wrap themselves around you when you're distracted, then wait until you breathe out to tighten their grasp. And with each exhalation they tighten even more until you can no longer expand your rib cage and you die by asphyxiation.

"What do you care?"

The Dreamer looks me straight in the eyes, and I can barely hold his gaze.

"Perhaps you need a hand. Some advice."

I remain silent. My eyes downcast. I stare at the pavement as if every inch of it has suddenly become interesting. There is someone inside me who is desperate for this, someone who wants to come out but instead remains holed up, defending himself, afraid to be seen as he really is because to surface would mean engaging with the person with ruffled hair and a cheeky expression. Plus it would involve a large quantity of water and salt in the form of tears. So I keep staring at the ground, scared that that someone might ooze out like toothpaste, too much and all at once.

The Dreamer waits in silence. He's in no hurry, just like everyone who puts you on the spot. In response I give him a taste of his own medicine.

"What would you do, sir, if your girlfriend died?"

And this time I stare into his eyes. The Dreamer scrutinizes me and remains silent. He stops eating. Perhaps he's never thought about this. Perhaps he feels bad. There, now he'll start to actually understand something and quit theorizing. He replies that he doesn't know and that he probably wouldn't be able to bear the burden of something like that.

He doesn't know. It's the first time that The Dreamer doesn't know something. It's the first time he's unsure of himself, that he doesn't dazzle like the Christmas window displays in town. He doesn't know.

"Well, sir, that's what I'm going through, and everything else has become worthless to me."

The Dreamer starts looking at the sky.

"Beatrice."

Silence. Then he asks me if that's the girl everyone is talking about at school: the girl who has leukemia. I lower my head, almost hurt by those words, which unfortunately are true: the girl who has leukemia . . . Silence. The silence of adults is one of the greatest victories imaginable. So I speak instead.

"She's not really my girlfriend, but it's as if she were. You see, sir, when I was talking to you about my dream, I was talking about Beatrice. I know that whatever my journey may be, she will be my companion on that journey, and if she's not on that journey, I no longer know which way to go."

The Dreamer remains silent. He places his hand on my shoulder and says nothing.

"She's so pale now. She's lost her red hair, the hair that made me fall in love with her. And I didn't even have the courage to speak to her, to help her, to ask her how she's feeling. I saw her in that state and I ran away. I ran away like a coward. I was convinced that I loved her, I was convinced I would travel to the four corners of the world with her, I was ready to do anything . . . I even gave blood, and then when I was in front of her, I ran. Like a coward. I don't love her. A person who runs away doesn't truly love. She was tiny, defenseless, and pale, and I ran away. I'm vile."

Those last words crush a concrete barrier that had slowly reinforced itself between my stomach and my throat; it shatters into fragments when it reaches my eyes, turning into tears that are as heavy and painful as stones. I bawl my eyes out with all the pain that I can, because it's good for me, almost like when I gave blood. I can cry and I don't know when it will happen again, even if I feel like a humongous idiot.

The Dreamer stands next to me in silence, with his strong hand on my shoulder. I feel like a fool. I am a sixteen-year-old guy and I am crying. I am crying in front of my history and philosophy teacher, with his mouth still covered in ice cream. Oh well, it's done now. The dam has broken and at the moment a million cubic yards of pain are flooding the world because of me, but at least it's no longer held inside.

After letting my tears flow for at least fifteen minutes—the fire of rage conceals at least twice the amount of salty water—The Dreamer interrupts the silence that follows, like the silence of sand after a violent storm.

"I'll tell you a story."

He says this as he hands me a vanilla-scented tissue.

"A friend of mine had argued with his father. He loved him very much, but this time he just lost his patience and told him to go to hell. In the evening as they sat down for dinner, his father had tried to speak to him, but he got up and left without saying a word. He didn't even want to listen to him. My friend had felt so strongly. He felt that he had won, that he was right. The next day his father's place at the table was empty. His father had had a heart attack, and that's how they'd parted. Without a word. But how could he have known? Since that day my friend has been unable to find peace because of that mistake. He's as ashamed of it as if he had committed the worst kind of murder. And do you know why he'll never forgive himself for having refused a goodbye to his father?"

I shake my head with a sniffle.

"Because his father, in a moment of rage, had said to him

that he was a loser, that he had chosen the job of a loser, despite the fact that the father had a well-established business that his son could have easily taken over. Tell me if that isn't something to be ashamed of and to run away from?"

It takes me a while to break the silence that follows his question.

"How did your friend get over it?"

The Dreamer kicks a discarded can on the pavement with anger.

"By living with it. By promising himself that he would not miss a single opportunity to fix a relationship that has deteriorated for more—or less—important reasons. There is always something one can do."

I already feel better. I, who in the face of an error would like life to have a rewind button. But life doesn't have one. Life goes on regardless, and it continues to play whether you want it to or not. All you can do is turn the volume up or down. And you have to dance. As best you can. But somehow I'm less frightened of it now. The Dreamer interrupts my thoughts.

"We all have something we're ashamed of. We've all run away, Leo. But that's what makes us men. Only when we have something written all over us that we are ashamed of do we start to have faces that are real . . ."

"Do you cry, sir?"

The Dreamer stays silent.

Then, "Every time I peel onions."

I burst out laughing, even if the joke is pathetic. I sniff and manage to hold back the tears I still have left to spill.

"It's normal to be afraid. Just as it's normal to cry. It doesn't mean you're a coward. To be a coward is to pretend nothing happened, to turn your back on things. To not care about any of it. I'm not surprised you ran away. I'm not surprised you're pissed off"—*He said "pissed off!"*—"with everyone and with yourself. It's normal. But getting pissed off"—*And again!*—"doesn't solve anything. You can be pissed off"—*That's three times!*—"as much as you like, but that won't cure Beatrice. I once read in a book that love doesn't exist to make us happy but to show us how strong our capacity to bear pain is."

A silent pause.

"But I ran away! I was supposed to be prepared to die for her so that she could get better!"

The Dreamer stares at me.

"You're wrong, Leo. Maturity is not shown by being willing to die for a noble cause, but by being willing to live humbly for it. Make her happy."

I still say nothing. Somebody inside me is leaving the cave. Someone who was hiding there, hurt and in need of help, is maybe finally convincing himself to face the dinosaurs. At this moment I am moving from the Stone Age to the Iron Age. Not a huge step, but at least I feel I have some sharp weapons against the dinosaurs of life. The feeling is stronger than the shield of iron and fire that I thought I had built with my anger. It's a different kind of strength, and this new somebody clings to my skin and makes it transparent, strong, elastic.

"It's late," says The Dreamer as I make an evolutionary leap of at least two thousand years.

He looks me straight in the eyes.

"Thanks for the company, Leo. And thanks especially for what you gave me tonight."

I don't understand.

"Sharing one's suffering with others is the greatest gift of trust one can give. Thank you for today's lesson. Today you were the teacher."

He leaves me standing there like a stupefied fool. He has already turned his back. His shoulders are thin but strong. The shoulders of a father.

I want to run after him and ask who his friend is, but then I realize there are things that are better left uncertain. My eyes are red from sobbing, I'm exhausted, drained, and yet I'm the happiest sixteen-year-old on earth because I have hope. I can do something to make things right: Beatrice, Silvia, friends, school . . . Sometimes the word of someone who believes in you is enough to lift your spirits again. I sing out loud, I'm not quite sure what. The people I come across take me for a madman, but I don't care and sing even louder when someone passes by, forcing them to rejoice with me.

When I go back home singing and with my face all puffy from crying, my mother glances confusedly at my father, who shakes his head and sighs. Why do parents think we're only okay when we look normal?

First: Silvia. This time I'm going to see her in person. None of this stupid texting. I'm going in person, with everything written—tattooed even—all over my face: "I am a poor fool. Forgive me."

I do something I've never done: I buy her a bunch of flowers. I feel awkward the entire time I stand choosing them under the canopy of the kiosk, knowing nothing about flowers. Eventually I opt for roses. An odd number. I've learned this much at least from one of Mom's magazines. I buy three white roses—the only exception to my fear of white—and I make my way to Silvia's block. I ring the buzzer. Her mother, probably unaware of anything, opens the door. Something is moving in the right direction. I go up.

I walk into Silvia's room, where she's listening to music with her headphones on and hasn't heard me come in. She looks up to find three white eyes looking at her and saying sorry. She's speechless. She takes off her headphones and looks at me sternly, then she smells the roses. When she looks up again, her blue eyes are smiling. She hugs me and gives me a kiss on the cheek. Not any old kiss. A kiss given by someone who is saying more with her lips than just greeting you. And you can feel the extra warmth that remains on your cheek. I sense it from the way she lingers for a moment before moving her lips away. She doesn't say a word. I just say, "Sorry." And I say it with words, without the risk that T9 might turn it into fear even though I do feel a little fear. But Silvia cares for me, and when someone cares, "sorry" never means "afraid."

I am happy, so happy that the white roses appear almost tinged with red, like those in *Alice in Wonderland*. "We'll paint the roses red; we'll paint the roses red . . . ," I sing to myself, like a child diving into a pool of Nutella.

My cast has already been off for a while, but it seems that my brain is still set in plaster because it won't budge. That's why I am studying with Silvia. Only she can help me catch up on all the school days I've missed. I don't want to ruin my summer by having to retake things. With Silvia I am strong. I am happy. But when I think about Beatrice, I continue to feel lost. After the umpteenth time of Silvia bringing me back to earth from one of my trips to the moon, she goes to get something out of a notebook she keeps in her room, one of those diaries that girls write their thoughts in.

In this sense girls are better than us. At least, Silvia is definitely better than me, because girls write important things down in their diaries. Every time they discover something important, they write it down, so that at any moment they can reread it and remember it.

I have tons of important things I'd like to remember, but then I never write them down because I'm lazy. So even though I know better, I forget them and always make the same mistakes, but I don't want to plunk myself down, my backside glued to the seat. That's what it means to have abilities but not apply them. To have a backside and never sit on it, which is the point of having it after all . . . If I had written down everything I've discovered, goodness knows how many things I wouldn't need to relearn each time. More than a diary, I think, a whole novel would come out of it. I think I'd enjoy being a writer, but I am not sure how to start, and besides, I'm easily discouraged because when I try to think about a story, I can never come up with a plot. Anyhow, Silvia has one of those diaries that helps you remember things. And slipped between the pages of that diary is a piece of paper.

"Here. This is the rough draft of the letter we wrote to Beatrice."

In that moment, my soul recomposes itself. As if by some kind of miracle all the pieces of paper that the river had swallowed up with my rage and cowardice are there in front of me, pieced back together by a miracle from Silvia, who saved those words.

"Why did you keep it?"

Silvia doesn't answer right away. She fiddles with the edge of the piece of paper, almost caressing it. Then, without looking at me, she whispers that she liked the words. She liked rereading them and hoped that one day her boyfriend would dedicate such beautiful words to her. Silvia searches my eyes, and for the first time I look into hers.

There are two ways of looking at a person's face. One is to look at the eyes as a part of the face. The other is to just look at the eyes, as if they *are* the face. To do it instills fear in you. Because eyes are life in miniature. White all around, like the nothingness in which life floats, then the colored iris, like the unpredictable variations that characterize a life, until plunging into the blackness of the pupil, which swallows everything like a dark well, a colorless and bottomless pit. And that's where I dive, looking at Silvia in that way, in the deep ocean of her life, entering it and letting her enter mine: through the eyes. I can't hold her gaze, but Silvia keeps looking at me.

"We can rewrite it if you want, and you can take it to Beatrice. We can go together, if you like."

Silvia has read my thoughts.

"It's the only way I could do it," I say to her with such a big smile that the edges of my mouth touch my eyes.

Then we start studying, and when Silvia explains things, it all becomes easier. Life makes more sense.

The Dreamer gives me an oral exam. I prepared for it with Silvia. Everybody expects a fight to the bitter end after the clash we had the other day, but nobody except Silvia knows that in the meantime there's been ice cream and a billion gallons of tears. Everything will go smoothly. The Dreamer and I are friends now. But then he asks me some really difficult questions, and I glare at him and say, "But that's not in the book."

Without flinching, he replies, "So what?"

I remain silent. He looks at me seriously and says he thought I was more intelligent, but I must just be a typical student who repeats things by rote and is thrown off by the first slightly different question.

"The most important answers are written between the lines of books, and you're the one who must be able to read them!"

Who do you think you are, Dreamer, to ruin my life and think you know everything and think that I care about the way you see things? You're the one who sees things like that and only you. Now quit breaking my balls and give me the same test as everybody else. I am on the verge of walking back to my desk and telling him to bite me when he says:

"Are you going to run away?"

So I think back to Beatrice and how I fled the hospital. Something happens inside me, and the man I evolved into a few evenings ago emerges from the cave. And so I answer. Not with the swear words of a capricious child. I answer as a man would. I get a nine out of ten, for the first time in my life. And that grade isn't about history. That grade is about *my* story, my life.

Beatrice is back home. The bone marrow transplant didn't go well. Her cancer isn't getting better, and her red blood keeps turning white in her veins. One of the most poisonous snakes on earth can make you die in atrocious suffering with its poison. A poison able to dissolve the structure of your veins. You start losing blood from your nose and ears, and your veins slowly liquefy until you are consumed.

That's what is happening to Beatrice. Beatrice, the most marvelous creature to exist on the face of the earth. Beatrice, who is only seventeen and had the most beautiful red hair known to history. Beatrice, the two most beautiful green windows in the galaxy. Beatrice, a creature who exists so she can carry her beauty across the world and make it a better place with her mere presence.

Beatrice is poisoned by this cursed white snake that wants to take her away. Why waste all this beauty? To make us suffer more. Beatrice, I beg you to stay. God, I beg you: Leave me Beatrice. Otherwise the world will become white.

And I will be left without dreams.

I'm seeing Niko again today. I remembered the hamburger dare we did once—who could eat the most Big Macs. It ended up 13–12 for Niko. Afterward we both threw up for three hours solid. I've never been so sick in my whole life. Every time we remember it we have fits of laughter. That's why we now only get the chicken nuggets.

Niko.

It came to mind because Niko has proposed a new dare: the winner is the one who scores the most goals in today's match against year 4C. The team is called Vitamin C, and they could certainly use some . . . We just need to win this game to catch up with Vandal's team and sail smoothly toward the final. There's just one tiny problem: I shouldn't be playing soccer yet.

There is only one solution in this case. To become the invisible man. I leave my radio on, close the door, stand on tiptoes, and silently escape to the soccer field. If my parents catch me, I'm done for. This time they would be the ones to break my arm and even my leg . . . But at least I'll get to play the match, and if I score a decent number of goals, I'll be back on track for the high-scorers' ranking. I have to at least get ahead of Vandal.

So here I am, with my shimmering cleats caressing the

third-generation grass as if it were a girl's cheek. Back on the field with Niko. He doesn't know everything that has happened to me in these past few weeks because I don't tell him everything like I tell Silvia. There's no need. Or perhaps I'm embarrassed. But on the field we're always the best. When we were little we both wanted to be like the twins from the *Captain Tsubasa* cartoon with their catapult trick, but neither of us had a twin. So when we met in high school, we realized that we were each the twin the other had always wanted. We never learned to do the catapult, but we did try once: I came out with a gargantuan bruise, and Niko banged his face against the goalpost.

But when it's crunch time we can triangulate in a way not even Pythagoras with his theorem could have imagined. We win hands down. I score five goals. We're tied with Vandal's team, and I am one goal behind him in the goal scorers' ranking. It couldn't have gone any better. I change clothes quickly to get home without being seen. Niko stops me.

"I've got a girlfriend."

He says this point-blank as he's taking off his Pirates shirt, and the news blends in with the smell of his sweat.

"Her name's Alice. She's in year 2, form H."

I rack my brain trying to visualize the girls from the second year, but I can't think of anyone named Alice.

"You don't know her. Her parents are friends with mine and I didn't know it. She showed up at my place for dinner one evening."

I'm curious to know what she's like.

"She's really hot. Tall, with long black hair, dark eyes. She also does track-and-field sprints. You should see her. When I hang out with her, everybody turns to look at us."

I say nothing. I'm unable to get excited by the news. Niko is too busy thinking about swaggering down the street with this hot chick next to him, and too taken by our victory to realize that I'm pretending to be curious and pleased for him. I'm suddenly jolted back into the hospital room where the most beautiful girl in the world is curled up like a wounded child—and all the beauty has been sucked away by a poisonous serpent, and that beauty not only will never be mine but will never be at all.

"I'm happy for you."

Niko wants to introduce her to me as soon as possible. I perfunctorily say yes, but in reality I hope to never see this so-called Alice.

"Have you seen the new FIFA video game? We absolutely have to crack it."

I nod with a forced smile as I watch Niko being sucked back into the Stone Age and into Alice's wonderland.

"Yeah, we should . . ."

It's all I can bring myself to say. The only thing I can focus on is the fear of losing Beatrice. I've never felt so alone after winning a match with my team of Pirates.

"It's a matter of life or death . . ."

"Come on, Leo, don't exaggerate. It's just a video game! Gotta go. Alice is waiting for me. See you tomorrow."

"See you tomorrow."

I slip the keys in the lock like a thief.

The door opens slowly. Nobody in sight. I hear music blaring from the radio. I recognize Vasco's voice repeating, "I want a reckless life, I want a life like those in the movies," and it comes across to me as a joke in bad taste. I close the front door. Mom hasn't heard me, but then Terminator starts barking frantically, gripped by the pressure on his bladder caused by his overexcitement whenever he sees me opening or closing a door. Mom appears, summoned by the commotion—and there I am, with my tracksuit and backpack, with Terminator yapping away as he circles me.

"What are you doing? Weren't you in your room studying?"

Leo, breathe. Everything is at stake here.

"Yes, but I needed a break. I took Terminator out to pee . . ."

The only excuse that can save me.

Mom stares at me like a police officer cross-examining someone in an American cop film.

"Then why are you so smelly?"

"I took a quick jog. I can't stand just studying and doing nothing else anymore . . . Sorry, Mom. I should have let you know, but Terminator was going nuts. You know what he's like!"

Mom's face relaxes. I make a dash for my room, where Vasco is still screaming, before my face betrays my lie and Terminator demonstrates, with proof, that nobody has taken his incontinent bladder for a walk.

Monday. It's five to eight. Five hours of classes await me, with an English test in the middle. A kind of gigantic cheeseburger with a slice of marble wedged in it. In the distance I see Niko with Alice, who indeed doesn't go unnoticed. They haven't seen me. I can't run into them. They're too happy.

I sneak away and hide behind a group of fourth years who, with the sports newspaper in hand, are checking the players' rankings to calculate the results of their fantasy soccer leagues. I've been following soccer much less lately. I'm caught up in other things, and I don't have time to watch every single program imaginable and every match of every championship taking place on a rectangle of green grass.

Anyhow, the image of Niko and Alice looking so happy together is too much for me this morning, and five hours of torture would only make things worse. I go back out into the street and slip down a quiet side road, so there is less risk of close encounters of any kind. Goodness knows why when you decide to skip school you inevitably run into people you haven't seen for centuries, especially Mom's friends who, coincidentally, will be having tea with her that afternoon.

Your son has grown so much, he's turned into such a

handsome young man . . . I bumped into him this morning in the park around noon . . .

Leaving aside the fact that to friends of moms everywhere, all kids grow into *beautiful young adults* . . . Mom plays along, plays down and pretends to be proud of the scoundrel who at noon should have had his butt glued to a green chair at school rather than sprawled out on a red bench in a park.

Enough of this. The die is cast, and render unto Caesar the things that are Caesar's, as Caesar said . . . At least, I think he said that. In the distance I hear the school bell ring, like the tolling of bells at a funeral. And I don't want to die. Each step that takes me farther away from school opens a chasm of fear and transgression that forces the ground to swallow me up. Why is going to school so difficult? Why do we have to do things when we are busy sorting out other more important things? And why is the English teacher walking toward me on this very street, the quietest in the entire school neighborhood?

I manage, just in the nick of time, to crouch over my tennis shoes, pretending to tie them while hiding behind an SUV that gives me cover. From the corner of my eye I see the teacher hurrying because she too is late and is so intent on rummaging for something in her bag that she doesn't notice my presence and walks right by. Phew! I breathe a sigh of relief, and a second later realize that my pretend shoe-tying was carried out on the early morning steaming pile from Terminator or some other dog . . .

My lucky day!

When you skip school you feel like a thief. And where do thieves go after a robbery? To their hideout. My hideout is the isolated red bench in the park near the river—the same one where I spent my first night as a tramp—beneath a huge tree with low and twisted branches that make it look like an umbrella with a million spokes.

On that bench, protected by that umbrella, I've conquered millions of beautiful girls, solved the trickiest problems of humanity, become a masked superhero, and devoured family-size bags of BBQ-flavored chips, which are in fact my favorite. Time passes very quickly under there, overtaking the calm flow of the river water. The secret of time is hidden on that bench, and all dreams can become reality.

And so today is the right day to apply myself (occasionally I do apply myself, but on my own terms) on my wooden bench, under the protection of the umbrella tree. I place my backpack in a corner and sprawl out with my knees bent. The sky is only blue in patches, crossed by crisp white clouds. They're not rain clouds but fresh sea clouds. This makes the blue even more intense. My gaze slips between the branches of the umbrella and, mixed with the color of the oval leaves, reaches out to the sky, where I see the image of my happiness emblazoned: Beatrice. Nobody pays attention to the sky until they fall in love. The clouds turn red and become her hair, spreading for thousands of miles, gently covering the world in a soft and fresh mantle.

I have to save Beatrice if it's the last thing I do, and I'm in the right place to do it. Only on this bench do dreams come true, so I fall asleep in the silence of the park. If we had the time and the right bench, happiness would be guaranteed. But unfortunately, somebody invented mandatory school.

I am awakened from my torpor by something brushing against my leg. I jump up, thinking it's some yucky grasshopper that has fallen from a branch. It's actually just my cell phone. Message from Jack: "The English teacher said she saw you this morning and you're not in class. I guess you're in trouble now." The punk is loving this. I really am in it! How come it's so hard to be happy, and the one time you're trying to solve this problem for good, someone stops you? Why didn't Silvia text me? Oh well, it is what it is.

I send a text to nobody, just to clear my thoughts. I write millions of text messages that I don't send, but they help me think. "I'm in my dream." Once again T9 surprises me. I set out to write *dream*, but it wants to turn it into *blaze*. "I'm in my blaze."

My bench could, at any moment, turn into a blaze, set on fire by all the people sickened by my heresies in life, as they did to heretics in the Middle Ages. They would tie me to the wooden bench and set fire to me under this marvelous sky, accuse me of being a coward, a weakling, a fugitive, a loafer, a sloth. And my dream would go up in smoke. But precisely because of this I must protect it. I must protect it from my parents and my teachers, from the envious, from my enemies and their fire. Today the wood of this bench is worth much more than the wood of my scrawled-over school desk.

I didn't skip school because I'm a sloth but because first I need to solve a more important problem: that of happiness. Even The Dreamer said, *Love doesn't exist to make us happy but to show us how strong our capacity to bear pain is.*

That's it. That's exactly what I'll say to my parents when they place me on the pyre of deserved punishment. I just wanted to love. That's all. I want to be cured of any drug: laziness, PlayStation, YouTube, *The Simpsons* . . . Can you understand that?

I pull out my penknife and start carving something in the trunk of the nearby tree. As I do this mechanically, I think about my next move, my checkmate on destiny, the move toward happiness. Occasionally I look up at the sky, and my fingers linger on the century-old creases of the tree that is strong, solid, and happy in the heart of that park. It is a tree and it acts like one; it sinks its roots into the water of the nearby river and grows. It follows its nature. That is the secret to happiness: being yourself and that's it. To do what you are called to do. I'd like to have the strength of that tree: rough and hard on the outside, alive and tender on the inside, where the sap runs. I don't have the courage to go see Beatrice. I'm scared. I'm embarrassed. I have myself, and it isn't enough. It's never enough. I continue carving the bark without thinking . . .

"What are you doing?"

I don't even look at the park ranger's face and reply:

"Scientific research . . ."

"Come on. You've never even taken science!"

It's not the voice of a warden. I turn around.

"Silvia?"

She looks at me with eyes I don't recognize. Silvia is really good at school. She's never unprepared, has never skipped a day, except for serious diseases like scurvy or leprosy and not for some generic condition indicated by a thermometer that has been warmed up on a lightbulb. Silvia is here, in front of me. Silvia is skipping school with me and because of me. Silvia would even come to find me in hell, just to make me happy. Silvia is a blue angel. I knew it. Or maybe she's an angel who looks like Silvia, who will punish me with her flaming sword for skipping school.

"We had a deal. We have to go and see Beatrice together. When I saw you disappear this morning, I knew you were coming here."

I make space on the bench where dreams come true.

"You too? I guess everybody saw me today. Have I been cast on *Big Brother* without knowing it?"

Silvia smiles. Then she stares at the bark on the tree. The trunk has been wounded by my penknife with a mathematical formula: H = B + L. Silvia turns serious, her face straining for a moment in a grimace of pain. But it quickly disappears and she says, "So, shall we go and solve the equation of happiness?"

Silvia is the lymph of my courage. Hidden but alive, she gives me the strength to overcome my limits. I take her hand.

"Let's go. There will be no blaze today. Just dreams."

Silvia looks at me, confused.

"Nothing, nothing. The genius of T9 . . ."

*Outside Beatrice's block I am overcome by the grasshopper syn-*drome: like in *The Blues Brothers*, where any excuse is good enough to run away. But Silvia is inflexible. She squeezes my hand tightly and we go upstairs. We are let in and we find ourselves in the living room, sitting in front of the red-haired lady I had first seen at the hospital and then in the photograph: Beatrice's mother. She knows Silvia, but not me. Fortunately. She tells us that Beatrice is sleeping. She's very tired. Her strength has diminished lately.

I tell her about giving blood, about the accident, and about everything else. She's a lady with a calm voice. Her face is tired and has aged, and her youthfulness in the photo seems to have stayed on the photographic paper. She offers us something to drink. As usual in these cases, I don't know what to do and accept. As we talk to her, I feel like I'm seeing Beatrice as an adult. Beatrice will be even more beautiful than her mother, who is a wonderful woman.

While she goes to get drinks, I try to memorize all the objects in their home. All the things that Beatrice sees and touches every day. A glass vase, a row of small stone elephants, a painting of a glistening marina, a bowl filled with iridescent and colored oval stones set on top of a glass table. I take one: it is every shade of blue, from early dawn to the dead of night. I put it in my pocket with the certainty that she must have touched it. Silvia glares at me with her piercing blue eyes. Beatrice's mother comes back.

"How come you're not at school today?"

Silvia says nothing. It's up to me:

"Happiness."

The lady looks at me, confused.

"Beatrice is paradise for Dante. So we came to see her."

Silvia bursts out laughing. I remain serious and turn red, almost purple. But when I see Beatrice's mother laugh, I start laughing too. I've never felt so ridiculous and happy at the same time. The lady smiles with a kindness that I've rarely seen on the face of an adult: only Mom smiles like that. Even her copper-colored hair, in parts shiny and in others opaque, appears to smile. She gets up.

"I'll call Beatrice now. Let's see if she's up to it."

I remain still, paralyzed with terror. I now realize what we are actually doing. I'm in Beatrice's home and am about to talk to her face-to-face for the first time. My legs aren't trembling; they're flapping like a flag, and my saliva has completely disappeared somehow, leaving my mouth feeling like a mini Sahara. I gulp down a sip of Coke, but my tongue stays as dry as firewood.

"Come with me."

I'm not even remotely prepared for this. I got dressed randomly. I have only myself, and I don't think it's enough. I'm never enough. But Silvia is here.

I find myself face-to-face with Beatrice's smile. It's a tired smile, but it's a genuine smile. Her mother left the room, closing the door behind her. I sit down in front of the bed, and Silvia sits at the end of it. Beatrice has a short layer of red hair that makes her look like a soldier, but she's still a perfect mix of Nicole Kidman and Liv Tyler. Her green eyes are green. Her face is worn but delicate and full of peace, with her gentle cheekbones and elf-shaped eyes. Her whole being is a promise of happiness.

"Hi, Silvia. Hi, Leo."

She knows my name! Her mother must have told her, or else she recognized me as the author of my text messages. Now she'll think that I'm stalking her, that I'm the loser who was trying to make it with text messages. Whatever the reason, she has pronounced my name—and that "Leo" coming from Beatrice's lips suddenly becomes real. Silvia takes her hand but stays quiet. Then she says, "He wanted to meet you. He's a friend of mine."

I'm on the verge of tears from sheer happiness. My lips are moving by themselves, despite not knowing what they should say:

"Hi, Beatrice, how are you?"

What an idiotic question! How do you *think* she feels, you moron?!

"I'm fine. Just a little tired. You know, the treatments are intense and they wear me out, but I'm okay. I wanted to thank you for giving blood. My mother told me all about it."

So it's true that my blood is nourishing Beatrice's red hair. I am happy. Extremely happy. The thin red hair that is growing back is thanks to my blood. My blood-red love. I think about this so intensely that I let something ridiculous slip out:

"I'm happy that my blood can flow in your veins."

Beatrice breaks into a radiating smile that could make a million frozen fish sticks defrost in a second. My heart rate doubles, to the point that my ears become hot and I think they have turned red too. I immediately apologize. I've said something ridiculous and tactless. What a fool! I want to disappear into the darkness of that room where I haven't yet set fire to anything because I'm so concentrated on Beatrice's face: the center of the sphere of my life.

"Don't worry. I'm happy to have your blood in my heart. So, you missed school today to come and see me. Thank you. It's been so long since I went to school. It all seems so far away."

She's right. Compared to what she's going through, school is a cakewalk. How can you be convinced at sixteen that life is school and school is life? That teachers are hell and holidays are heaven? That grades are the final judgment? How can it be that at sixteen the world has the diameter of the schoolyard?

Her green eyes dance on her pearly face like fires in the

night, revealing a gush of life inside her like a mountain spring, hidden, silent, and full of peace.

"I'd like to do so many things, but I can't. I'm too weak. I get tired so fast. I dreamed of learning new languages, of traveling, of playing an instrument, but no. Everything has gone to pieces. And my hair . . . I'm embarrassed to be seen like this. Mom had to persuade me to let you come in. I've even lost my hair, the most beautiful thing I had. I've lost all my dreams, like my hair."

I look at her and I don't know what to say. In front of her I have become a drop of water that evaporates in the August sun, and my useless words are breaths that dissipate in the air. And as timely and inappropriate as the school bell, I say:

"It will grow again, as will all your dreams. One by one."

She smiles wearily, but her lips are quivering.

"I hope so, I hope so with all my heart, but it seems like my blood won't decide to get better. It just keeps rotting."

A pearl in the shape of a tear flows from Beatrice's left eye. At that point Silvia strokes her face and wipes the tear away as if Beatrice were her sister. A moment later she too leaves the room. I'm left alone with Beatrice, who half closes her eyes, through tiredness and concern about Silvia's reaction.

"I'm sorry. Sometimes I use words that are too strong."

Beatrice is worried about us, and it should be the other way around. I'm alone with her now and have to share with her the secret of her road to recovery. *I am your cure, Beatrice, and you are mine. Only when we both know this and agree will anything be possible, forever.* I concentrate on telling her

I love her. I prepare myself within, as if my body is an athletic track, but I feel like my back is against the wall. *I love you. I love you. I love you. Just three words. I can do it.* Beatrice can tell I'm struggling.

"We shouldn't be afraid of words. That's what I've learned through my illness. Things must be called by their name, without fear."

That's why I want to tell you what I am about to tell you . . . That's why I am about to scream out that I love you.

"Even if that word is *death*. I'm no longer scared of words because I'm no longer scared of the truth. When your life is at stake, you get sick and tired of roundabout ways of saying things."

And that's why I must tell her the whole truth, and now. The truth that will give her the strength to get better:

"There's something I'd like to tell you."

I hear these words coming out of my mouth and I don't know where that sentence came from or who had the courage to pronounce it. I don't know how many different Leos there are inside me, but sooner or later I'll have to choose one. Or perhaps I'll get Beatrice to choose the one she likes best.

"Tell me."

I stay silent for a minute. The Leo who had the courage to say the first sentence has already disappeared. He should say "I love you" now. I find him hidden in a dark corner, his hands covering his face, as if something horrific is about to attack him, and I convince him to speak. *Go on, Leo, come out of there, like a lion coming out of the forest. Roar!*

Silence.

Beatrice waits. She smiles at me encouragingly and rests her hand on my arm.

"What is it?"

Her touch turns into a rush of blood and words.

"Beatrice, I . . . Beatrice . . . I love you."

My face takes on the typical expression you have during an oral math test, in which you fumble along and hope the teacher makes some gesture to let you know whether you're getting things right or not, so you can backtrack as if you had said nothing. Beatrice's fragile hand, as white as snow, is resting on mine like a butterfly. She keeps her eyes closed a few moments, then takes a deeper breath and reopens them.

"It's lovely of you to say that, Leo, but I don't know if you've quite understood. I'm dying."

Like a hurricane of swords, that piercing cluster of syllables leaves me bare in front of Beatrice: bare, wounded, and defenseless.

"It isn't fair."

I say it like someone waking up in the middle of a dream after a long night, when he is still unable to distinguish reality from nighttime. I whispered the words, but she heard them.

"It's not a question of fairness, Leo. Unfortunately it's a fact—a fact that has happened to me. The question is whether I'm ready for it or not. And I wasn't before. Now, perhaps, I am."

I'm not following her anymore, I don't understand her

words. Something is rebelling inside me and I don't want to listen. Is my dream taking me back to reality? The world has definitely turned upside down. Since when do dreams show you reality? Something invisible is thrashing me and I am left without defenses.

"All the love I have felt around me in these past few months has changed me. It has allowed me to touch God. Little by little, I have stopped feeling scared, stopped crying, because I believe I will close my eyes and I will reawaken near him. And I will stop suffering."

I don't understand her. In fact, she's making me really mad. I climb mountains, I cross oceans, I submerge myself in white up to my neck and she rejects me like this. I did everything possible to have her, and when she's within reach I find out she's miles away. My fingers clench into a fist, and my vocal cords tighten up, ready to scream.

Beatrice draws closer and holds my clenched hands, which soften as my vocal cords relax. She has warm hands, and I feel life flowing out of my fingers as they stroke hers, as if through our hands we could exchange souls, or as if our souls can no longer find the boundaries within which to contain themselves. She then lets my hands go, delicately, giving time for the soul to return into its shell, and I can feel her sail off again, far away from me, toward a harbor I don't know.

"Thanks for visiting, Leo. You should go now. I'm sorry, but I'm really tired. I'd like you to come and see me again though. I'll give you my number, so you can let me know if you're coming. Thank you."

I'm so confused and stunned that I act without thinking. I play dumb, though in truth I already have her number, but as she says it out loud I realize it's different from the one Silvia gave me awhile back. I can't ask questions, but all those unanswered messages are now clearer. Beatrice doesn't think I'm a loser, then, and her silence wasn't on purpose! I still have some hope. Maybe Silvia made a mistake, maybe she has the wrong number too, or somehow I wrote it down wrong. My memory for numbers is worse than my ninety-five-year-old grandmother's. I bend down and kiss her on the forehead. Her delicate skin has a subtle scent of soap, none of that Dolce & Gabbana or Calvin Klein stuff. It's her smell, and that's it. Beatrice, and that's it. No cover-up.

"Thank *you*."

She lets me go with a smile, and when I turn toward the door I feel a white giddiness behind me that wants to chew me up and swallow me.

Beatrice's mother thanks me and tells me that Silvia is waiting for me downstairs. I make an effort to seem relaxed.

"Thank you, ma'am. If you don't mind, I'd like to come and see Beatrice again. And if you need anything, please count on me. You can call me anytime . . . even in the mornings."

She laughs openly.

"You're a smart guy, Leo. I will."

When I walk out of the front door, Silvia is there waiting for me, leaning against a streetlight as if wanting to become part of it. She keeps her eyes fixed on mine, which barely see her as they float in pools of tears. She holds my hand, and as fragile as leaves, we walk in silence for all the remaining hours of the day, hand in hand, each finding strength not from within, but in giving strength to the other.

When I get home, my mother is sitting in the living room. My father is sitting beside her. They look like two statues.

"Sit down."

I put my backpack between my legs to defend myself from the fury that will be unleashed at me in a moment. My mother is the first to speak.

"School called. You're at risk of failing. From today until the end of the school year, you're not leaving the house."

I look at my father to figure out if it's one of Mom's usual speeches that then leaves room for a series of negotiations until it is reduced to withholding my allowance or getting grounded for a Saturday. But my father is dead serious. End of conversation. I say nothing. I pick up my backpack and go to my room. What do I care about this kind of punishment? If need be I'll sneak out, and there's no way they can keep me at home. And what can they do if I sneak out? Punish me for a year? I'll just keep sneaking out until they punish me for life, at which point it would be pointless to add any more punishments because they would all overlap. I lie on my bed. My eyes stare at the ceiling, where Beatrice's face appears like a fresco.

I don't know if you've quite understood. I'm dying.

Her words pierce my veins like a thousand needles. I haven't understood anything about life, about suffering, about death, about love. Me, who thought that love could conquer everything. How deluded. Like everyone: we all recite the same script in this comedy, only to be destroyed at the end. It's not a comedy; it's a horror story. As I turn to stone on my bed, I realize my dad has come into my room. He's looking out the window.

"You know, Leo, I skipped school once too. My classmate's brother had just been given a convertible Spider, and that morning we went to the seaside to try it out. I still remember the wind muffling our shouted conversations and the motor that pierced through the air like a bullet. And then the sea. And all the freedom of the sea that seemed to be ours. Everyone else was shut between the four walls of school and we were there, fast and free. I still remember that horizon, vast and without reference point, where only the sun was a limit to infinity. At that moment I realized that what was important when faced with the freedom of the sea was not having a ship to sail it, but a place to go to, a harbor, a dream for which it was worthwhile to cross all that water."

My father stops talking, as if through the window he can see that horizon and the lights of a distant harbor, like in a dream.

"If I had gone to school that day, Leo, I wouldn't be the man I am today. I got the answers I needed on a day I didn't go to school. A day in which, for the first time, I searched for what I wanted by myself, at the cost of being punished . . ."

I don't know if my father has turned into Professor Dumbledore or Dr. House, but he has understood exactly how I feel. I can hardly believe it. I had to seriously misbehave to get to know who my father is . . . It's the first time he tells me something about his past. I mean, I've known him for about sixteen years, yet I know very little about him—almost nothing that really counts. I'm about to say something, but it's so cheesy I'm appalled, and fortunately Dad continues.

"I don't know why you didn't go to school today, and you deserve punishment for it because that's part of owning up to one's responsibilities. I don't know why and I don't want to know. I trust you."

The world is changing. I wouldn't be surprised if any minute now it started turning in the other direction, or if Homer Simpson became an exemplary husband, or if Inter Milan won the Champions League. My father is saying the most incredible things. It's like a movie. The exact words I need. I wonder why he didn't do it sooner. A timely reply arrives without my having to formulate the question.

"I now realize that you're willing to risk a whole year for what you consider important, and I am sure it isn't trivial."

I remain silent, wondering how it can be that skipping one day of school is enough to change your life from black and white to color. First Beatrice, now Dad. All I manage to say is, "How were you punished that time?"

My father turns toward me with an ironic smile.

"We'll talk about that too. I have two or three tricks to teach you for avoiding certain beginners' mistakes."

I smile back. And that smile between Dad and me is the smile between one man and another. He's about to leave the room and the door is closing when I find the courage:

"Dad?"

He pops his head back in, like a snail.

"I'd just like to be allowed to visit Beatrice. I was with her today."

Dad looks serious for a moment, and I prepare myself for his *Don't even think about it.* He lowers his gaze to the floor and then looks up again.

"Permission granted, but only for that reason. Or else—"

"You'll reduce me to the dust of my shadow," I interrupt. "I know. I know."

I smile an almost perfect smile.

"And Mom?"

"I'll talk to Mom."

The door has already closed when he says it.

"Thanks, Dad."

I repeat it twice. The words roll on the floor while I, stretched out on my bed, watch the white ceiling turn into a starry sky. My blood pumps quickly through my veins and sets them on fire. For the first time after a punishment I don't hate my parents or myself. And the dust of my shadow is stardust.

Not being allowed to leave the house until the end of school means I have over two months of seclusion awaiting me, except for my visits to Beatrice, which Mom has ratified as an addendum to our armistice. Despite my punishment I am happy, because the only truly important reason for going out has been granted. As for the soccer tournament, I'll think of something . . . And besides, the good thing about this punishment is that I'll probably end up passing the year. With no distractions and not being allowed out, my occupations have become: studying (mostly with Silvia, who applies herself even though I don't); spending time on my computer (but in this case too following a schedule determined by the pact of March 21—that is, the day I visited Beatrice and got punished); reading books, or rather, reading one book, the umpteenth book that Silvia has lent me, called *Someone to Run With*, and at least the title isn't bad even though it's about a dog being taken for walks (what a torment!); playing the guitar (occasionally Niko comes over and we play a couple of songs together . . . In the meantime he's broken up with Alice, or actually, Alice ditched him for someone else); and, incredible as it may sound, looking at the stars.

Yes, looking at the stars, for the simple reason that Dad has infected me with his passion for astronomy. He knows all the names of the constellations and he can recognize stars, creating invisible silver cobwebs with the tip of his finger that join them up, like the dot-to-dot puzzles in newspapers.

This may come in handy with Beatrice one day. I want to show her all the stars and invent a constellation for her with her name. What shape will it have? What shape does a dream have?

I walk into Beatrice's room with my guitar slung over my shoulders. I feel like one of those buskers who meanders through the subway cars, who ends up begging for a little happiness.

Beatrice smiles: I've kept my promise. She is lying facedown on her bed reading, while Elisa is playing on the stereo, her voice bouncing off the walls and looking for a way out through a crack in the partially closed window.

"So today we start!" says Beatrice, her smile spreading all the way to her green eyes, as if we are about to begin something that is destined to never end.

"I want to learn to play this song," she says, nodding toward the stereo.

"I have waited a long time
For something that isn't there,
Instead of watching
The sun rise . . ."

"With a teacher like me it won't be a problem. I'll have to come every day though."

Beatrice laughs with her heart in her eyes, throwing her

head back and putting her hand over her mouth, as if wanting to limit a more open gesture than what she should allow herself, she who could allow herself anything she wanted.

"I'd like that, Leo, but you know I can't manage it . . ."

I take my guitar out of its case as if I were The Edge.

I sit on the edge of the bed, near Beatrice, who pulls herself up. I'd like to capture the scent of her movements in a smell recorder, if such a thing existed. I position the guitar on her legs and show her how to hold the handle, which appears a bit oversized next to Beatrice's fragile body. My arm guides her from behind to help her find the correct grip, and for an instant my mouth is so close to her neck that I wonder what my brain is waiting for to order my lips to kiss it.

Elisa's song ends.

"There, now you have to keep the string pressed down against the fret, putting pressure with your thumb from behind and then plucking the string with your right hand."

Beatrice's lips are pursed in an effort to make a sound come out, a sound that remains dull in the now quiet room, the dull sound made by her weakened body. Her body, which should be filling the world with unheard harmony and an infinite symphony, instead produces nothing but a clumsy note. I place my hand over hers with a delicate pressure. Our hands overlap like mine did when I prayed as a child.

"Like this."

The strings start to vibrate.

With my body I am allowing Beatrice's to play.

Beatrice stares at me and smiles as if I have shown her a

treasure that had been hidden for centuries, yet I have simply taught her how to pluck a guitar string.

She hands me the guitar impatiently.

"Show me how you do it. That way I'll learn quicker."

I take the guitar as she sits back, curling up and hugging her knees with her arms. I start strumming the chords of Elisa's song. Beatrice recognizes it and closes her eyes in search of something lost.

"Why don't you sing?" she asks me.

"Because I don't know the words," I answer quickly, but the truth is that I am embarrassed to sing out of tune.

With her eyes closed, Beatrice opens her lips slightly, and a fragile voice flows from her vocal cords like a freshwater spring.

"And miraculously
I can't avoid hoping.
And if there's a secret
It's to do everything as if
I only saw the sun . . ."

My fingers become part of her voice that flows over them as if they had become the riverbed of that vocal flow of water. Her song fills every corner of the room, even those that the light never reaches. It shines out of the window, floating around the sleepy city—numbed by its gray and repetitive bustle—softening the right angles of daily life and jaws clenched by pain and fatigue.

"A secret is
To do everything as if,
To do everything as if,
You only saw the sun,
You only saw the sun,
You only saw the sun
And not something that isn't there . . ."

I accompany the last words with a final arpeggio.

We sit in silence, the silence generated by the end of the song: silence doubled, squared even, where the song lyrics echo like a lullaby that has cradled pointless worries to sleep and reawakened things that count.

Beatrice opens her eyes and smiles. The world has been painted in the green of her eyes and the red of her hair and the gold of her smile.

Then Beatrice cries, her smile mixing with tears.

I watch her closely, my eyes fixed and still, wondering why pain and joy cry in the same way.

The afternoons I spend studying with Silvia constitute, in some cases, the only antidote to the venom of sadness. We study, and occasionally one of Dante's verses or a philosopher's saying carries us far away. I tell her about my visits to Beatrice. I recount everything we say to each other and I feel better: my encounters with Beatrice have lodged inside me like a stone to be digested. But digesting stones is impossible. In a way my chats with Silvia act as the enzyme to help break them down. Silvia listens to me attentively, without comment. Even her silence is enough. Though one time she asked:

"Should we pray for her?"

I trust Silvia, and if she thinks something is right, I do it. So occasionally we say a prayer. Not that I believe in it, but Silvia does. And so we say this healing prayer for Beatrice:

"God, *if you exist*"—I add this bit secretly—"make Beatrice better."

It's not much of a prayer, but the gist is there. And if God is God, he doesn't need too many words. If God doesn't exist, those words are pointless; but if God does exist, maybe he will wake up from his long slumber and for once get around to doing something worthwhile. I've never said this to Silvia, to not offend her, but it's what I think.

Beatrice. I go to her place every week. The day always changes according to how she is, because some afternoons she's too tired. There have been no improvements. After the latest blood transfusions her situation is stationary. Either Beatrice or her mother sends me a message when she's feeling better, and I shoot off to her house on public transportation. (My Batscooter is defunct since the accident and I doubt it will be reincarnated into anything. And anyhow, even though the damage was covered by insurance, the pact of March 21 states that any discussion of possibly acquiring a new means of transport can only be held after successful completion of the year.)

Each time I take something that might serve as a distraction for Beatrice. When I go into her room, my aim is to give her a piece of paradise (in a metaphorical sense, because I don't believe in paradise), but then I find paradise there, because she is there (so maybe paradise does exist, because such splendid things surely cannot end). One time I take her a CD with my favorite song on it.

"Will you dance with me?" she asks me in a faint voice. I can't believe it. I hold Beatrice's fragile body in the light of her room, and I make her float slowly like a bubble that from one moment to the next could drift away in the air. Her hair has grown back enough to smell its fragrance. I squeeze her hand and her waist: a crystal glass that could shatter any moment, even because of the red liquid I want to pour into it.

The urge to sleep with her that I once associated with the thought of her is now distant. Beneath her light clothing her body seems to be part of mine, as if our skin no longer knows which bones and which muscles to cover. Her face, resting in the hollow of my neck, is the missing piece to the disjointed puzzle of my life, the key to everything, the center of the circumference. Her feet follow my steps, which are inventing the choreography designed by the first dance between a man and a woman. It feels as if my heart is beating everywhere, from the tips of my toes to the most northern strand of my hair, and the strength that I find within would be enough to create the entire world inside this room.

Beatrice only manages a few steps before she abandons herself in my arms. As light as a white snowflake. I help her back into bed. I turn off the stereo. She briefly looks at me with gratitude before closing her eyes, overcome by tiredness, and in that single gaze that closes down, I realize I have everything that she is losing: my hair, school, dancing, friendship, family, love, hope, a future, life . . . But I don't know what I'm doing with any of these things.

I can't study and tomorrow I have a math test. I keep seeing Beatrice's gaze as it turns off, defeated.

I see it behind the lines,

between the lines,

in the white of the lines.

It's as if my senses have withdrawn and developed another form of perception: everything that Beatrice is losing I have to live not only for myself, but for her too. I have to live it twice. Beatrice likes mathematics. And now I want to study it, and study it well, because Beatrice is even sad about having to give up that mysterious drivel . . .

At Beatrice's house I always turn into a new character: first the guitar teacher, now the geography teacher. Who would ever have thought it—me, who has never studied geography and has done nothing but match the names of countries to their metallurgical and steel industries, which, by the way, I've never understood the difference between, not to mention the sugar beet fields, which I imagine as full of plants with the sugar packets you get in cafés hanging from them.

I come and see Beatrice and each time I take her to a new city. Beatrice dreams of traveling, and when she gets better she wants to travel the world, learn its languages, discover its secrets. She already knows English and French; she wants to learn Portuguese, Spanish, and Russian. I wonder why Russian, with those unfathomable letters. Isn't Greek enough?

She says that knowing other people's languages helps you see the world better. Every language has a different point of view. The Inuit, for instance, have fifteen words for *snow*, based on temperature, color, and consistency—whereas to me snow is snow and that's it. Then you add an adjective to figure out if you can snowboard on it. The Inuit see fifteen different kinds of white in the white I see, and that's something that terrifies me.

I collect material studying the customs and traditions of a city or nation. I search for images on the internet of the most beautiful places to visit, of monuments not to be missed, perhaps linked to interesting stories. I prepare a PowerPoint presentation and then we look at it on the computer while I pretend to take Beatrice around those streets, as if I am an expert tourist guide.

In this way we have visited the Golden Ring in Russia, wrapped up in a thousand layers of wool to protect ourselves from the cold; we have rested in the gigantic shadow of Christ the Redeemer, who looks over Rio; we have lingered in silence in front of the Taj Mahal in India, an extraordinarily white building that sits on red sand, built by an Indian king as a token of love for his wife; we have dived into the waters of the Great Barrier Reef after stopping by the Sydney Opera House; we have taken part in a tea ceremony, possibly the first tea I've ever drunk in my life, in an unforgettable corner of Tokyo.

We still want to cruise along the Danube and see an Icelandic geyser; eat Sicilian cannoli on the seafront; take a black-and-white photo on the Seine; stroll along Las Ramblas looking at all the artists; hug the Little Mermaid; steal dust from the Acropolis; buy clothes in the Big Apple and wear them in Central Park; cycle along the canals of Amsterdam, making sure to keep our balance so we don't fall into the water; knock down at least one of the Stonehenge boulders; scramble along the edge of a Norwegian fjord with the risk of being swept away; and stretch out in an immense Irish field thinking that only two colors exist in the world: green and blue . . . We have the whole world to discover and explore, and Beatrice's room turns into all these places, thanks to our super-low-cost tours.

"Beatrice, where do you want to go in the summer after you finish high school?"

Beatrice says nothing and looks up, placing her finger on her nose and mouth like someone searching for a difficult answer.

"I'd like to go to the moon."

"To the moon? A mass of white dust without gravity, immersed in the darkest silence that exists . . ."

"Yes, but all things that are lost on earth are stored there."

"What do you mean?"

"Don't you know the story of Astolfo in *Orlando Furioso*? He's a knight who sets off to retrieve common sense for Orlando, who has gone crazy for love, so that he can return to fighting."

I shake my head and imagine myself as a frenzied Leo who has lost his mind for love.

"You'll study it. But it's just a fantasy," adds Beatrice, almost sadly.

"What would you go and retrieve?"

"What about you?" asks Beatrice.

"I don't know, maybe my first guitar. I left it in a hotel in the mountains and never got it back. I was attached to it because I had learned to play with that one. Or maybe my old scooter . . . I don't know. You?"

"Time."

"Time?"

"The time I have wasted."

"Wasted how?"

"With pointless things . . . time I didn't use for others. I could have done so much more for my mother, for my friends . . ."

"But you still have your whole life ahead of you, Beatrice."

"It's not true, Leo. My life is now behind me."

"You mustn't say that. You don't know . . . You can still get better!"

"Leo, my surgery went badly."

I'm left speechless. I can't imagine the world without Beatrice. I can't bear the silence that would exist. All the cities to visit would instantly disappear, pointless beauty if I were alone. Everything would lose its meaning and would become white like the moon. Only love gives meaning to things.

Beatrice, if we had fifteen ways to say I love you—like the Inuit do for snow—I would use them all for you.

Outside Beatrice's house the May light drips down on me, like the shower water after soccer matches with Niko. And when I turn the water off, I've already made it to Silvia's house for the dreaded, never-ending Italian revision before the big test on the whole second-semester syllabus.

We carry on until late. It's already eleven when her mother timidly comes into the room to ask if we want something to drink. While we sip a glass of Coke that wakes us up a bit, Silvia suggests we go out on the balcony to get some air. The Milky Way seems to have given itself a polish for the occasion. I start showing Silvia some of the constellations. I repeat what Dad has taught me, possibly adding a few creative details . . . I point to the stars that are almost invisible in the glare of the city lights and that make up my favorite constellations: Perseus, Andromeda, and Pegasus.

I tell Silvia, who slowly moves her gaze from my fingertip to the sky as if I am drawing the sky myself, the story of Perseus defeating Medusa despite her petrifying gaze, from whose blood the winged horse takes flight, as white as the foam of the sea: Pegasus, who still floats freely along the Milky Way. Perseus, who runs into Andromeda, imprisoned on a rock, waiting for a sea monster to devour her, and frees her. He frees her from the monster.

"My father made me realize that the sky is not a screen. I used to think of it like a television, with a few colored dots scattered here and there on its surface. Instead, if you look at it carefully, the sky is like the sea. It's deep. You can almost perceive the distances between stars, and it's scary to think of how tiny you are. And you fill that depth of fear with stories. You know, Silvia, I didn't realize it, but the sky is *full* of stories. I couldn't see them before, but now I read them like a book. My father taught me to see the stories—otherwise they slip away, they hide, they stretch out like invisible threads of a plot between one star and another . . ."

Silvia listens to me, staring at the luminescent dots on the uniform backdrop. Next to her the smell of the city lessens and even the streets seem scented. Silvia has peace in her heart. Silvia smiles.

"People are a bit like stars: maybe they shine far away, but they shine, and they always have something interesting to say . . . But it takes time, sometimes lots of time, for those stories to reach our hearts, like light to our eyes. And anyhow, you also need to know how to tell stories. You're good at it, Leo, you put passion into it. Perhaps one day you'll become an astrophysicist or a writer."

"An astro *what*? No, I can't tell the future . . ."

"What are you talking about, you dope? An astrophysicist is someone who studies the sky, the stars, the celestial orbits."

"Who knows . . . Maybe I'd like that. But I guess there's

too much math to learn. Although the Milky Way is one of the few white things that doesn't terrify me."

"How come?"

"Maybe because the whiteness is actually made of lots of small bright dots that are linked to each other, and each of those links holds a story to remember."

"I guess only beautiful stories deserve constellations . . ."

"You're right. Look at how Perseus frees Andromeda and Pegasus glides about white and free."

"It takes some imagination, but—"

I interrupt Silvia's words, which float in the clear air up to the stars. It almost seems like the stars can hear us.

"I'd like to free Beatrice from that monster, like Perseus did. And fly away on a winged horse."

"It would be nice . . ."

"Do you think I could be a writer too?"

"Tell me a story."

I remain silent. I stare at a flickering star that is redder than the others.

"Once upon a time there was a star, a young star. Like all young stars she was tiny and white like milk. She seemed fragile, but it was only the effect of the light she radiated that turned her into pure light, almost transparent. They called her Dwarf because she was small. White, because she was bright like milk: White Dwarf, Dwarf for short. She loved wandering around the sky and meeting other stars. With the passing of time, Dwarf grew and became red and large. She was no longer Dwarf but Giant, Red Giant. All the stars envied her beauty and her red rays, like infinite strands of hair. But the secret of Red Giant was to remain Dwarf within. Simple, radiant, and as pure as Dwarf, even if she appeared giant and red. For this reason, Red Dwarf continues to flicker in the sky, from white to red and vice versa, because she is both. And there is no beauty more beautiful than her in the heavens. Or on earth."

I turn silent. My story is not a story. There is no story, but only what was suggested to me by a glowing star. I point to the star.

"I want to dedicate that star to you, Silvia."

A white and red smile lights up Silvia's face, as if her face is a mirror capable of reflecting the glow of her star from millions, perhaps even billions, of light-years away.

Silvia leans her head on my shoulder and closes her eyes. And I stare silently at Perseus, Andromeda, and Pegasus. The sky has turned into a huge dark cinema screen, about to show all the movies we could wish for, while something small and bright nestles soundlessly in a corner of my heart, like a grain of sand hiding in an oyster waiting to become a pearl.

"I love you," Silvia's eyes say.

"Me too," say mine.

My Italian teacher gives me an oral exam and asks me why I only just started studying. I look at Silvia who is gently shaking her head, and I swallow the words I am about to say—but I know who I must thank. Only one thing goes badly in the test: I get my subjunctives wrong.

"Why do you get all your subjunctives wrong, Leo? It's almost like you do it on purpose. Even the simplest ones."

Again I say nothing and curse the day when, to be accepted by the group I hung out with in middle school, I decided to give up the subjunctive case because none of them used it. You can give up the subjunctive to be part of a gang, but not if you want to speak Italian. And so I get a seven instead of an eight.

Tomorrow I'm going to start repeating sentences with the subjunctive, whether I like it or not. There, I just did it. I like it, even if it means having to correct it in everything I write. If I want to become a writer, I need to learn to use the subjunctive tense. Sure, the subjunctive isn't essential to life, but thanks to it you live better: life becomes filled with nuances and possibilities. And this is the only life I have.

I go see Beatrice, and she's writing in her diary. Like Silvia does. She greets me with a smile and asks me to help her write. Nobody reads her diary, but she will give me permission if I write it for her.

"If you help me write I'll let you read it," she says, and it feels like I'm stepping into the room that holds all the world's secrets.

It has a red cover and white pages. White and unlined. The worst thing that could happen to me . . .

"Beatrice, I can't write on unlined pages. I might spoil everything."

I say this while staring at Beatrice's immaculately tidy handwriting. The date in the upper right-hand corner and the thoughts formulated in her delicate, elegant, and precise handwriting. It looks like a white dress on a windy day in spring. I read the paragraph that she's writing: "Dear God . . ."

What does she mean, "Dear God"?! Yes: "Dear God . . ." Beatrice writes letters to God. Her entire diary is made up of brief letters to God, in which she describes her days and confides in him with her fears, joys, sadness, hopes. I reread the last part of today's letter out loud because she asks me to, so we can pick up from where she had left off.

"I'm really very tired today. I'm struggling to write to you, yet there are so many things I'd like to say. But I take comfort in the fact that you already know everything. Despite this, I still like telling you about things. It helps me understand them better. I wonder if up in the sky I will be able to have my red hair again . . . If you made my hair red, it's because you liked it like that, full of life. So maybe I will get it back."

As I read, my voice is on the verge of cracking, but I manage to stop myself.

"Now, Leo, you can write: 'I was getting really worn out by writing today, and my hand was hurting. Fortunately, you sent me Leo, one of your guardian angels.'"

I've never thought of myself as a guardian, let alone an angel, but I don't dislike the thought at all. Leo the guardian angel. It sounds good. In the meantime Beatrice has stopped to think. She stares blankly, her green eyes appearing like a forgotten seabed from which an ancient treasure is about to emerge any moment now. I interrupt her trance.

"Are you happy, Beatrice?"

She continues staring into space and, after a pause, says, "Yes, I am."

When I look up from her diary, she has drifted off to sleep. I stroke her and it feels like I am stroking her weakness. She doesn't notice. She's sleeping. I sit there looking at her for half an hour without saying a word. By looking at her I see beyond. I sense something that frightens me because I am unable to give it a name. I read over what we wrote. This time it is me who has made someone's soul visible. Beatrice's soul, with my skewed, slanted handwriting . . . Every line I have written points downward. I only realize that now. I don't know how to write on a white page. It's as if the words were rolling down a cliff until shattering.

Then her mother comes in and I leave. She kisses my forehead and I, not knowing what to do, give her a hug. From the way she thanks me, I realize I have done the right thing. Since I've been trying to live for Beatrice too, I seem to have come up with all sorts of good things. This too is love, I guess, because afterward I'm happy—and the secret to happiness is a heart filled with love. I'll take Terminator out for a pee today, even if I have to do it for the rest of my life. Beatrice can't, but I can. This too is life.

If Beatrice writes to him, God surely must exist.

I waste time writing my MNS (messages never sent) on my cell phone. The truth is that T9 is smarter than me. T9 can think of seventy-five thousand words and I can only think of a thousand. And it's true. There are so many words I don't know, can't think of, words I've never heard of and that T9 suggests to me. I don't know if the plural of *luggage* has an *s* or not, but T9 knows. I don't know if *conscience* has an *i* in it, but T9 knows. I don't know if *acceleration* has one *l* or two. And when I want to cuss out someone, by the fourth letter it has changed the word to something else, forcing me to reconsider and find a less offensive synonym.

Who invented T9 anyway? Goodness knows how much money they made with it. I should also invent something that will make me a load of money. Maybe if I applied myself more I could do it. Maybe not. And if I write a novel I'll write it using T9. Why do I waste time thinking about stuff like this?

Whatever it is, I find myself having written—goodness knows how—"Dear Fin" because the word *God* doesn't come up on T9. And to me *Fin* doesn't seem a bad nickname for God. The name *God* scares me. I carry on writing, just like I did with Beatrice, except at least the lines stay straight on my cell: "You say you are our father, but you seem a bit too laid back up there in heaven. I don't know your name, so if you don't mind I'll call you Fin, because that is what T9 calls you. I can't accept your will because what you are doing to Beatrice makes no sense. If you are almighty: save her. If you are merciful: make her better. You put a dream in my heart: don't take it away from me. If you care about me: show it. Or are you too weak to be Fin? You say you are life, but you take life away. You say you are love, but you make love impossible. You say you are truth, but the truth is that you don't care about me and you can't change things. It's no surprise then that nobody believes in you. Perhaps I'm being presumptuous, but if I were in your place, the first thing I'd do—and you don't need to be Fin to get this—is to make Beatrice better. Amen."

A message interrupts me as I'm writing and I read it out loud.

"Always remember that I'm here. I care about you, even though you don't deserve it. ;-) S."

Silvia is an angel and is in direct contact with God, so maybe I should ask her if she has Fin's cell phone number so I can send him the message. Fin, I'm sure that you'll make Beatrice better! I would if I were in your place, and I hope you're better than me . . .

I'm back at Beatrice's. I was beginning to get worried, but then her mother sent me a message. I find her asleep, thinner, opaque. An IV counts the passing seconds, drop by drop. She opens her eyes and her smile seems to come from somewhere far away, the way old people smile, with melancholy.

"I'm so tired, but I'm happy you've come. I wanted to write in my diary, but I can't hold my pen. I feel like such an idiot."

I pull a piece of paper out of my pocket and secretly put it behind the page I must write on: a piece of lined paper to write straight lines on the white page. When I want to, I really do apply myself! I write what Beatrice dictates. Occasionally she stops, her voice breaks, she has shortness of breath. Then she dozes off. I wait and watch her drift away like a boat without a motor, without a sail, without oars, carried by the current. She opens her eyes again.

"I am too tired . . . You tell me something, Leo."

I don't know what to talk about. I don't want to tire her with my nonsense. I tell her about school and about my struggles, about what happened this year, about The Dreamer, about Gandalf, about Niko, and about the soccer tournament that the Pirates are about to win. I tell her about Silvia, about the times she saved me from trouble, about the day she skipped school with me and then encouraged me to come and see her . . . Then Beatrice suddenly interrupts me.

"Your eyes shine when you talk about Silvia, like a star . . ."

Beatrice can say incredible sentences with the simplicity of a child asking for yet another cookie. I remain silent like someone who has been subjected to great injustice but can do nothing to defend himself. I can't love Silvia. I can and want to only love Beatrice, yet she is the one telling me that my eyes shine like stars when I talk about Silvia.

"Have you ever fallen in love, Beatrice?"

She answers yes with a gentle sigh and says nothing. I realize it would be inappropriate to ask her anything else, but I also know that only she has the right answers.

"And what was it like?"

"It was like a home to go back to whenever I wanted. Like when you go scuba diving. Down there everything is still and motionless. There is absolute silence. There is peace. And maybe when you resurface the sea is rough."

I listen in silence and get the feeling that the words I've used in my life need to be reexamined for their definition of *love*, even though as things currently stand if I search for that word the only thing written there is "see under Beatrice." While I'm absorbed in these pointless thoughts, Beatrice becomes startlingly drowsy, as if fading. Or perhaps she's just keeping her eyes closed, but I realize that it's time for me to go.

Silvia is blue, not red. Yet my eyes shine in her blue.

When you don't know the answer to a question, there's only one solution: Wikipedia. However, Wikipedia says nothing about whether Silvia could be more than a friend to me. The question plagues me like the summer cicadas and I can't drive it away. I try to split the question in two. Does Silvia love me? Do I love Silvia? I take at least eleven tests on Facebook to find out if someone loves you. The result is clear-cut: Silvia does everything with me that a person in love does, but who doesn't have the courage to say it. My turn now. But I don't want to find out with a test. It's too important. I need to verify in person.

"Silvia, can we study together? I need help with Greek poets."

Poetry definitely has no purpose. It is just an excuse to fall in love.

While Silvia is repeating the translation of some very difficult verses by Sappho—"Immortal Aphrodite, on your intricately brocaded throne"—I stare at her without listening to the words, following the movement of her lips.

"And you, O Blessed Goddess, asked what had happened this time, why did I call again, and what did I especially desire for myself in my frenzied heart . . ."

I follow the waves of her black hair fluttering as she pronounces the words. Wings of a seagull effortlessly gliding in the wind.

"Come to me now once again and release me from grueling anxiety. All that my heart longs for, fulfill . . ."

I stare at her blue eyes, full of life and attention for me. For the second time I don't look *at* her eyes, but *into* her eyes. I dive into a calm and refreshing blue sea.

"What's the matter, Leo?"

I shake myself out of the reverie I had plunged into without realizing and from which I have no desire to be awakened.

"You seem distracted. Your eyes are shining. Are you thinking about Beatrice? Let's take a break . . ."

I wake up from a dream.

"No, no, carry on. I'm listening."

Silvia smiles with understanding. "Okay, now comes the part I like best, the one about the red apple. Concentrate: 'Like a sweet-apple turning red high on the tip of the topmost branch. Forgotten by pickers: not forgotten, they couldn't reach it.'"

As Silvia repeats and follows the Greek words with her finger, I—for the first time—think I understand that dead language.

I learned these verses by heart and repeated them until the break of dawn—which I'd never yet seen—caught me in love, in crazy-red love. But how can I betray Beatrice? How can I reach Silvia, so perfect? Yet it is Beatrice who opened my eyes, who made me see what I wasn't seeing. Silvia is home. Silvia is peace. Silvia is shelter. Will I ever be able to reach you, Silvia?

The worst thing about life is that there's no instruction manual.

With a cell phone you follow the instructions, and if it doesn't work, there's the warranty. You take it back and they give you a new one. Not so with life. If it doesn't work, they don't give you a new one. You're stuck with the one you have—used, dirty, and malfunctioning. And when it doesn't work you lose your appetite.

"Leo, you haven't eaten anything. Are you sick?" asks Mom. It's impossible to hide anything from her.

"I don't know, I'm not hungry," I answer dryly.

"You must be in love then."

"I don't know."

"What do you mean, 'I don't know'? Either you are or you aren't . . ."

"I'm confused. It's like I have a million-piece jigsaw puzzle without the complete picture to start from. I have to do it all myself."

"But that's life, Leo. You build the road as you go along, with the choices you make."

"But if you don't know how to choose?"

"Try to find the truth and choose."

"And what is the truth about love?"

Mom says nothing. I knew it. There's no answer, no instructions.

"You must search for it in your heart. The most important truths are hidden, but that doesn't mean they don't exist. They are just harder to find."

"And what have you found out in all these years, Mom?"

"That love doesn't want to have. Love just wants to love."

I don't answer. I start eating again while my mother washes the dishes in silence.

My phone is on the table, next to my glass. I pick it up and send Silvia a message:

"Tomorrow, I mean today, at five o'clock at the bench. I want to talk to you! It's a matter of life or death."

I get there half an hour early to practice by heart the speech that I want to make. A homeless guy approaches to ask me for some change and I, feeling generous with the world because I am about to declare my love to Silvia, give him a euro. Two, in fact. He says to me:

"God bless you."

As soon as I see her approaching, I wonder how I could have been so blind for so long. She tells me what a wonderful place this is and that everyone should have a place like this to plan their dreams and share their secrets. I beckon her to sit down with all the respect I would have for a queen, and as I wring my hands in search of words, she stops me with the utmost seriousness.

"I want to say something first, Leo."

I very much hope it is the same thing, so we can get it over with and hug each other.

"I no longer want to keep this heart-wrenching secret."

Here we go. Once again, Silvia saves the day.

"Beatrice never answered your messages because I never gave you her number."

I look at Silvia like someone who has just landed from Mars and sees a human being for the first time. Her beautiful features suddenly appear rigid, made of papier-mâché, like an empty mask.

"I know, Leo. I'm sorry. It's my fault."

I don't understand.

"That time you asked me to give you her number? I just pretended to do it."

I remember noticing, when Beatrice gave me her number, that it didn't match the one I had. The love-filled words I had prepared vanish like the "I love you" messages written in the sand near the seashore.

My tone of voice becomes as hard as ice.

"Why did you do it?"

Silvia remains silent.

"Why did you do it, Silvia?"

Silvia replies mixing words with tears.

"I was jealous. I wanted you to send those messages to me. But I never had the courage to tell you. I kept your letter to Beatrice for months imagining that it was for me. I was terrified of losing you. Forgive me."

I sit in a white silence, similar to the one on the moon. She stares at the river's current and doesn't have the courage to raise her gaze. I get up and walk away, leaving her there, like a perfect stranger. Silvia is no longer anyone for me. Love cannot come from betrayal.

"I want to forget you as quickly as possible."

I repeat it through my tears. And that thing that a few nights earlier had nestled in a corner of my heart dries up into a grain of salt that comes out in my tears, dissolved, lost forever.

I am tired of being betrayed.

I have so much pain clenched in my chest that I could burn down the world. Being holed up at home fuels my fire. I can't stand it any longer, so I go to my father's study and tell him outright.

"Dad, enough. I get it. That's enough now!"

He looks at me without saying a word. He remains silent. I provoked him, I yelled at him, and he says nothing. What kind of way is that to react to provocation?

I slam the door and go back to my room. I turn the music up until the windows are shaking, so that everyone can hear me and nobody can talk to me. I want to close myself away in a house of noise, because today the house I live in is not mine. Terminator starts whimpering like he does in these situations. He always whimpers whenever he hears Linkin Park at full blast and whenever my mother cooks chicken with peppers. It's as if they rekindle his primordial instincts or bad memories from his puppyhood. Terminator really is a weird dog. If I have to be reincarnated, I hope I don't end up being Terminator. I wonder who Terminator was in his past life.

I turn up the music up and the lyrics from "Numb" are on the verge of shattering the windowpanes, so that everyone can hear me. Suddenly Mom screams, "Leo, turn it down! I can't even talk on the phone!"

That's exactly what I want, but you don't get it and think I enjoy listening to this music at full blast. Do you think I care? I just want to fill this world with my noise while I plug my ears.

Then my father walks into my room. He says nothing. I turn the volume down.

"Let's go for a walk."

He's heard me. My father has heard me. He has heard what I was really saying.

We don't talk about anything. But with Dad near me I feel almost calm, my doubts about everything and everyone subsiding. My wounds burn less. Dad, Father. How do you become a father? You have to read lots of books, have at least one child, and have godlike strength.

I will never be capable of that.

We lie next to each other with our eyes closed after five minutes of deep silence. It's a game that Beatrice taught me. The silence game: a few minutes of silence, eyes closed, staring at the colors that appear beneath your eyelids. Occasionally I cheat and look at her just a few inches from me, holding my breath so that she can't tell I've turned my head.

"Don't open your eyes," she says, sensing something.

"I'm not."

"What do you see?"

"Nothing."

"Concentrate."

"What do you see?" I ask her curiously.

"Everything I have."

"What color is it?"

"Red."

"And what is it?"

"It's the love I receive. Love is always a debt. That's why it's red."

I don't get it. I'll never get things at Beatrice's level. Ever.

"And you, Leo? What do you see?"

"White."

"With your eyes closed?"

"With my eyes closed."

"And what is it?"

". . ."

"Well?"

"Everything I don't have. Love is always a credit that will not be repaid."

"Oh stop it," Beatrice says, laughing and giving me a kiss on the cheek.

After today, I'm never washing my face again.

The time has come to settle the score: the final showdown against Vandal. The match that will determine the winner of the tournament. We are one point behind them. All we can do is win. All we *must* do is win. There is much more than victory at stake here: revenge for Niko's nose, the goal scorer's ranking, and the Pirates' pride. I feel the right kind of rage. Rage that explodes into fiery shots that scorch the skin of our opponents and turn into wounds on Vandal's legs.

We're laying everything on the line. A year of hard work. If you win the tournament, the girls recognize you and you become cool. "The Pirate. There he is, that's the Pirate. The captain of the Pirates . . ." I can already hear them. How I wish Beatrice could see me play. I want to dedicate the game to her, the victory, the goals, the triumph over Vandal. Now I just have to focus. Half an hour still to go but I've been ready for at least three. Niko is coming to pick me up on his scooter.

Text message. It'll be Niko telling me to head downstairs and wait for him there. "I'm frightened . . . I'm tired, extremely tired. I'm alone . . . Beatrice."

I call her.

"What's up, Beatrice? What's going on?"

Her voice is broken. She's crying, crying like I've never heard her cry.

"I'll be right there!"

I go downstairs, and when Niko arrives I don't give him time to breathe.

"Give me a lift. Now. I'll meet you later, I hope I make it . . ."

Niko is speechless and drives off, leaving me at Beatrice's alone. I see him speeding away, his scooter making the sound of a friend who is leaving forever.

And that sound is excruciatingly painful.

Beatrice opens her eyes, red from crying, and pulls back from my embrace.

"Thank you for coming. I couldn't have gotten through today alone."

"What do you mean?"

"I'm frightened."

"Of what?"

"Of losing everything, of ending up in a void, of silence, of disappearing, and that's it . . . of no longer having the people I love near me."

There isn't a single acceptable word or sentence in my head. The only thing that comes out is the last remaining truth, like those trees you see standing alone in a field of green.

"I'm here."

I squeeze her hands as if I could tear her away from the emptiness of fear, like a trapeze artist entrusted with his partner's life as it's suspended in the air, without a safety net.

"Write . . ."

Her muttered words are confused, and I have to bend my ear to her lips to understand them. Her breath is warm and her words are as rough as a piece of iron being dragged across stone. I write the words that Beatrice whispers to me in a sigh. When she has finished dictating, she hands me her diary.

"Take it. Keep it. As of today I'm not writing anymore. It's for you."

I can't take it. I shake my head and place it near her.

"I thought I was writing it for myself. Then I realized I was writing it for you. It's what I can and want to give you, Leo."

I don't resist.

"Beatrice, one day we'll read it together."

She smiles at me.

"Yes. Go now. It's getting late. I'm tired."

I want to give her something too, but I haven't brought anything with me. I can't just leave like this. I rummage in my pockets. Nothing, except . . . the stone with a thousand shades of blue that I took from her living room. How embarrassing! But it's the only thing I have. I place it in the palm of her hand, as if it's a diamond.

"My lucky charm. I want you to keep it."

Beatrice smiles with the sky in her eyes.

"Thank you."

I kiss her red hair and in one second my life is filled with her blood.

"See you next time."

"See you next time."

I clutch Beatrice's diary tightly to my chest as if it's my skin. I think again about the fact that the only thing I was able to give her was something I stole from her home. I have nothing to give, if not the love that I receive or steal. Before leaving Beatrice's house I steal another blue stone. I can't go around without a lucky charm . . .

Night is the place for words.

The words in Beatrice's diary have shone like daylight in my first night without sleep, my first night of being alive: my first night.

If heaven exists, Beatrice will take me there.

> The pain forces me to close my eyelids, to hide my eyes. I always thought that I would devour the world with my eyes, that like bees they would rest on things and distill their beauty. But my illness is forcing me to close my eyes: because of the pain, because of exhaustion. Only little by little did I realize that with my eyes closed I could see more, that from beneath my closed eyelids I could see all the beauty of the world, and that beauty is you, God. If you are making me close my eyes it is so that I pay more attention when I reopen them.

This is written in Beatrice's diary. And today I'll close my eyes and look at life through hers. If life had eyes, it would have Beatrice's. Starting today I want to love life as I've never loved it before. I'm almost ashamed not to have started sooner.

I get back from school. Mom opens the door for me.

"What's for lunch?"

She looks at me as you would look at a wounded child.

"Oh no, not minestrone . . ."

I tell her I got an eight in philosophy, but even before I've specified the subject she hugs me tightly, hiding my face in the hollow of her neck.

I can smell Mom's fragrance, a fragrance that as a child brought me comfort: a scent of rose mixed with lemon. Subtle. But she's not hugging me because of the grade; otherwise her tears wouldn't be moistening my face. Only then do I realize.

I'd like to free myself, but she won't let go of me, so I sink my fingers into her flesh to understand if what she is telling me without saying a word is true.

My mother is the only woman I have left.

The only skin I have left.

Beatrice is dead.

That's the word for it. No point in beating around the bush. She wouldn't have wanted that. People say she has departed, passed away, left us.

Beatrice is dead.

The word *dead* is so violent that you can only say it once and then you have to be silent.

Silvia is the only person I'd like to talk to, but I don't have the strength to forgive her for lying to me. Life is a test to get a truth out of you that you don't know but that you'll pretend to remember just to avoid any more suffering . . . to the point you end up believing that lie, forgetting that it was you who made it up in the first place.

God, the stars are no longer needed. Turn them off one by one.

Dismantle the sun and wrap up the moon.

Empty the ocean, uproot the plants.

Nothing is important anymore.

And most of all, leave me alone!

The church is bursting with people; the whole school is there. Everyone is gathered around a shiny wooden shape that hides her body, her lifeless eyes. The Beatrice I remember no longer exists and the one that is now inside that wooden box is another Beatrice. There lies the mystery of this thing called death. But what I loved in her and about her hasn't floated away. It hasn't slipped off like a single hurried breath. I clutch her diary tightly between my hands, like a second skin.

Gandalf is celebrating the mass. Once again. He talks about the mystery of death and tells us the story of a guy called Job from whom God took everything. Despite this, Job remained faithful to him, even though he had the courage to reproach him for his cruelty.

"And as Job screams out among his tears, God says to him: 'Where were you when I laid the earth's foundation? Who shut up the sea behind doors? Have you ever given orders to the morning, or shown the dawn its place? Does the rain have a father? Who gives birth to the frost from the heavens? Who provides food for the raven? Does the hawk take flight by your wisdom and spread its wings toward the south? Speak out if you have so much wisdom!' "

Silence falls after Gandalf's reading.

"We, like Job, are today crying out our disapproval to God; we do not accept what he has decided to do, we do not accept it, and this is only human. But God asks us to have faith in him. This is the only solution to the mystery of pain and death: faith in his love. And this is divine, a divine gift. And we must not be afraid if we cannot do that now. Indeed, we should say this clearly to God: We will not stand for it!"

Nonsense! Forget faith, I hate God. Gandalf continues, unflinching.

"But we have the solution that Job did not have. Do you know what the pelican does when its nestlings are hungry and it has no food to offer them?

"It gashes its breast with its long beak until nourishing blood flows out for its chicks, who will drink from that wound like a fountain. Like Christ did for us. And it is because of this that he is often represented as a pelican. He defeated the death of children, hungry for life, with his blood, his indestructible love, for us. And his gift is stronger than death. Without this blood we die twice . . ."

Everything turns silent inside me. I am a rock of pain suspended in the vacuum of love. Completely impenetrable.

"Only this kind of love overcomes death. He who receives it and gives it does not die, but is born twice. Like Beatrice!"

Silence.

Silence.

Silence.

"I now invite up anyone who wishes to remember her."

A long, awkward silence follows, then I get up, under everyone's gaze. Gandalf watches with apprehension as I approach. He's worried I might say something foolish.

"I just wanted to read the last words in Beatrice's diary, words that she dictated and that I wrote down. I'm convinced that she would have wanted to make them known to everyone present."

My voice cracks and I swallow unstoppable tears, but I continue reading anyway.

"Dear God, today Leo is writing to you because I can't manage it. But even though I feel so weak, I want to tell you that I'm not afraid, because I know that you will take me in your arms and cradle me like a newborn baby. The medicines haven't cured me, but I'm happy. I'm happy because I share a secret with you: the secret of seeing you, of touching you. Dear God, if you hold me in your arms, death no longer scares me."

I look up and the church seems flooded by the Dead Sea of my tears on which I float in a boat that Beatrice built for me. My eyes meet Silvia's, and she's staring at me and trying to comfort me with her gaze. I look down. I move quickly away from the microphone because, despite my wooden raft, I too am about to drown in tears. The last words I remember are those of Gandalf's:

"Take this and drink from it, all of you. It is the blood I have spilled for you . . ."

Even God wastes his blood: an infinite downpour of blood-red love that falls on the world every day in an attempt to make us alive, but we remain deader than the dead. I have always wondered why love and blood are the same color: Now I know. It is all God's fault!

That rain doesn't touch me. I am impermeable. I remain dead.

Last day of school. Last hour. Last minute.

The bell rings: the last one.

A cry of freedom accompanies the cackle, as if prisoners are suddenly being freed from their life sentences after being granted clemency from goodness knows who.

I'm left alone in class. It's like a cemetery in here. The seats and desks that have been alive for a whole year, animated by our fears and follies, wounded by our pens and pencils, sit there as still as gravestones. A deadly silence shrouds everything. The blackboard still bears signs of The Dreamer's hurried scribbles, wishing us nice holidays in his way:

"He who awaits attains what he was waiting for, but he who hopes attains what he wasn't hoping for."

A phrase from Heraclitus.

As far as I'm concerned it's a farce. I have lost everything in which I laid my hopes.

So the school year goes out like a firework. This year has lasted a lifetime. I was born on the first day of school, then grew up and old in just two hundred days. Now the almost universal judgment of grades awaits me, and then I hope that holiday paradise can begin. I will pass the year, with reasonably good grades.

There is one thing I have realized, though, thanks to Beatrice: I can't afford to throw away a single day of my life. I thought I had everything and I had nothing, the opposite of Beatrice, who had nothing and yet she had everything.

I've had nothing more to do with Niko and the others. The Pirates lost the tournament because of me. I never explained what happened. I don't care. I don't care at all. Silvia has given me a letter, but I'm not opening it. I don't have the courage to suffer anymore.

BeardFace, the janitor, peers in and finds me sitting there, motionless, staring into space.

"In three years I've never seen you be the last to leave. What's up? Have you flunked the year?"

"No, I was just thinking."

"Well then, it's a miracle!"

We laugh together, and a pat on the back is enough for me to come back to life.

Halfway down the corridor, I turn back and shout out to him:

"Don't erase it!"

School is the world back to front: nothing is written black on white, but vice versa. At school everything is designed to be forgotten, like the flimsy white dust of chalk.

BeardFace doesn't hear me, and with the chalk duster, protagonist of so many battles, relentlessly wipes over the hopes of a dreamer.

After the Summer

Then crying, alone in my lament,
I call on Beatrice and say: "Are you dead?"
And while I call on her, it comforts me.

DANTE ALIGHIERI, *VITA NOVA*, XXXI

Summer is the reason for living, but this one has been different.

It hasn't been a time of commotion, but one of silence. I didn't see or hear from anybody for the entire summer. I spent nearly three months in the mountains, in the hotel that we always go to. This is the first year I actually wanted to go. I needed silence. I needed to walk alone. I needed to not make new friends. I need to not find a girlfriend at all costs, just to have something to tell Niko after the holidays. I needed Mom and Dad. I needed Beatrice's diary because in there I found a glimmer of happiness. I needed the bare minimum, and in the mountains that's easier to find.

In the mountains, at night, you can see the stars like nowhere else. Dad often tells me stories about the stars. Mom sits there listening, looking at us more than the stars. One evening Dad tells me the story of the star I gave to Silvia and that light, still warm, irradiates a corner of my heart that I had shut away with a thousand locks.

I haven't been able to open Silvia's letter. I didn't even bring it with me. I keep writing her text messages, but I can't bring myself to send them. But I save them all: filed under MNS.

Just as I save all the ones she has sent me in the past. I can't bring myself to delete them. I must have over a hundred of them on my phone, and occasionally, when I don't know what to do, when I'm not thinking about anything, when I'm bored, when I need to, I reread them randomly. I skim through and choose the message number that most inspires me. Thirty-three: "You're the stupidest guy I know, but at least you're not boring." Twelve: "Remember to bring your history book, idiot!" Fifty-six: "Stop being a fool. Let's go out and you can tell me everything." Twenty-one: "What's your shoe size? What's your favorite color?" One hundred: "Me too."

The best message: I could fill it with whatever I wanted and it would always say "me too." I was never alone. It was number one hundred and it brought good luck. I could write a novel with just text messages. For now there are only a few protagonists: Silvia, Niko, Beatrice and her mother, The Dreamer, and me. Yes, The Dreamer. I had his number, and over the summer I sent him a message to say hello and to ask him if his friend, the one with the problem with his father, was feeling better. He replied that thanks to Beatrice's words that I read at the funeral, his friend's wound had started to heal. I then asked him how his friend knew about Beatrice. Had he invited him to the funeral?

"In a way . . . Thank you, Leo. I'm happy to have met you."

I reply, "But what for?"

Can one have such conversations via text? Yes, I'm convinced of it.

"For having the courage to read those words. We will meet those we have loved again, and we have our whole life to ask for forgiveness."

I read that reply at least a hundred and twenty-seven times. It was too philosophical, but by the hundred and twenty-eighth time, I realize three things:

1. I call all "things" that are truly important *philosophical*, and perhaps that's what philosophy is for.
2. I must answer The Dreamer's message: "It's thanks to Beatrice. See you soon!"
3. I can't wait to go home and read Silvia's letter.

I spend the evening looking at her star, then Mom comes and sits next to me in the heart of night, with the scent of fir trees and the moonlight shining on her rested face.

"Mom, how can you love when you don't love anymore?"

Mom keeps gazing at the sky. Now she is lying next to me as I stare at the White Dwarf Red Giant known as Silvia.

"Leo, love is a verb, not a noun. It's not something established once and for all, but it evolves, it grows, it goes up and down, it becomes submerged like the rivers hidden in the earth's core, but that never interrupt their journey toward the sea. At times they leave the ground dry, but they still flow beneath the surface in dark cavities and, from time to time, they resurface and gush out, nourishing everything."

The sky appears to resonate with those gentle words, which only on a night like this don't sound rhetorical.

"So what do I have to do?"

Mom says nothing for at least two minutes, then her words emerge from the silence like a river that after a great deal of effort reaches the sea.

"You should love anyway. You can do it all the time: to love is an action."

"Even when it means loving someone who's hurt you?"

"But that's normal. There are two types of people that hurt us, Leo. Those who hate us and those who love us."

"I don't get it. Why would those who love us hurt us?"

"Because whenever love is involved, people sometimes behave stupidly. Perhaps they do things the wrong way, but they are still trying . . . You should worry when those who love you stop hurting you, because it means they have stopped trying or that you have stopped caring."

"And if you still aren't able to love?"

"You haven't tried hard enough. We often get things wrong, Leo. We think that love is in trouble, but it is actually love itself asking to grow . . . Think of the moon: You only see a sliver sometimes, but the moon is always there in its entirety, with its oceans and its peaks. You just have to wait for it to grow, for light to slowly illuminate all the hidden surfaces . . . and that takes time."

"Mom, why did you marry Dad?"

"Why do you think?"

"Because he gave you a star?"

Mom smiles, and the moonlight glistens on her perfect teeth, framed by a face that can calm my every storm.

"Because I wanted to love him."

Mom ruffles my hair to free the sullen thoughts that are still lodged inside me, like she used to do when I was a child filled with fears and hiding in her arms.

Then there is nothing but the complete silence of those who gaze at the moon and the sky and speak to whomever they want to, there beyond the stars.

Where did I put it? I can't find it. I can't find it anywhere.

Cosmic disaster. School starts the day after tomorrow and I can't find Silvia's letter. Fin, help me out—at least this time! Then I saw the light: my history book. Thank goodness I didn't sell it like the others, just to avoid upsetting The Dreamer who sees so much in that book, more than what's actually written in it.

That's where I'd left it, but I don't want to read it yet. My dreams come true on a park bench, and that's where I want to read it and think about things calmly.

"Mom, I'm taking Terminator out for a pee!"

I run, run, run. I run like I've never run in my life. Terminator drags his tongue on the ground, collecting all the dirt in the universe. He can't keep up with me. It's as if between the two of us Terminator is the one taking me for a walk and trying to slow me down.

There it is, my bench: empty, solitary, red, waiting for my dreams. I let Terminator wander about on his own because he's also happy here and behaves.

I open the letter and see Silvia's handwriting, the handwriting I've always wanted to have and never will.

Dear Leo,

Here I am writing to tell you about something that made me think of you and that I couldn't stop myself from sharing. I know you're livid with me and that you don't want to talk to me. Take this letter as an outburst that only you can help with.

The other day I went on a trip with a group of family friends. Suddenly I found myself on my own with the son of one of them. His name is Andrea and he has a crush on me. When we were left alone, he came up to me and tried to kiss me. I pushed him away and he was stunned. He turned around and walked off like you did that day. But as I stared at Andrea's back, I couldn't find the strength inside me to feel bad. Andrea means nothing to me. When I stared at your back that day, from your bench, something inside me broke. I realized that I can only imagine the world with you.

The Greeks claimed that man was originally spherical and that Zeus, as punishment for his wrongdoings, had broken him in two. The two halves wander around the world looking for each other. Nostalgia drives them to keep searching, and when they find each other that sphere wants to be reunited. There is some truth in this story, but it isn't quite enough. When the two halves meet again, they have lived their own lives up until that moment. They are not the same as they were when they first separated. Their edges no longer fit together. They have flaws, weaknesses, wounds. It's not enough just to meet again and recognize each other. They must now choose each other too, because the two halves no longer match perfectly and only love leads to accepting the sharp edges that don't line up, only an embrace can soften them, even if it hurts. That day, Leo, I realized that our halves don't match perfectly and only an embrace can make us fit together. Without your presence, the world has become empty. I miss everything about you: your laughter, your gaze, your wrong subjunctives, your text messages, your conversations. All those trivial things that mean everything to me, because they are yours.

There. That's all I wanted to tell you. Your back will never be like anybody else's to me. When you turn your back on me, it's life turning its back on me. Forgive me. And if you can, take me back with my flaws. Embrace me as I am. As I will embrace you. Our embraces are what will change us. I love you as you are, and hope you can do the same, even if I am not perfect like Beatrice. I would like your bench to become ours: two hearts and one bench. As you can see, I don't need much . . .

I look up and the river is flowing, indifferent to global changes, this river that has collected centuries of tears, joy, and pain, carrying them to where tears should be—in the sea, which is salty precisely for this reason. I clutch my lucky charm that glistens blue in the blue of the morning, and I feel Beatrice near, so near that it's as if I'm living with two hearts, mine and hers, with four eyes, mine and hers, with two lives, mine and hers.

And life is the only thing that you can't deceive if you, heart, have the courage to accept it . . .

It's evening already. One of those September evenings when scents, colors, and sounds are like a rainbow that can join earth and sky. Beatrice is looking at me from her star. I have my guitar in hand and an ancient dachshund at my feet: Terminator was the necessary excuse to leave the house at this time of night without arousing too many suspicions. I ring the buzzer and ask her to look out of her bedroom window.

"Who is it?"

When she leans out from the second floor of what has become a fairy-tale castle by now, she can barely make me out in the darkness of the dimly lit street. But she can hear my voice.

"When you wrote out that letter for me, I promised I'd sing for you . . ."

Silence. As I tune my guitar I get carried away by the dark blue of the sky and start singing:

> *"You know*
> *In this way are born*
> *The fairy tales I'd like to have*
> *In all my dreams—*

And I will tell them
So that I can fly to heavens I don't have
And it's not easy to be left without fairies to catch
And it's not easy to play if you're not there . . ."

In the darkness I imagine Silvia's face as she listens, listens to my voice, and I no longer feel embarrassed about anything, because if I have a good voice, it's so I can give it to her:

"Take me with you
Among angelic secrets
And devilish smiles
And I will turn them
Into tiny gentle lights
And I will always manage to escape
Among colors to be discovered . . ."

I'm immersed in all the world's fairy tales and am reinventing them in an urban context to make them real. More faces appear at the windows of the enchanted building, intrigued by that serenade. But I don't care. I'm like the freest of men prepared to face the entire world just to avoid losing what really counts.

"Air, breathe in the silence for me,
Don't ever say goodbye,
But lift up the world . . ."

My voice feels free and heavy at the same time. Its heaviness caused by past events that have, however, been transformed into wings and feathers that allow it to soar, light and earnest at the same time. Only now that I am burdened can I fly.

> *"Air, embrace me.*
> *I will fly, I will fly, I will fly,*
> *I will fly . . ."*

Silence. When I look up, Silvia is gone. Somebody whistles and somebody boos at me. Somebody laughs, maybe out of envy. Somebody claps.

The door of the enchanted castle opens. A shadow slowly walks toward me. I stare at the face approaching me in the semidarkness.

"Silvia is at her dance class. I told you from up there, but you couldn't hear me. She should be back anytime now. You're good though! I listened carefully. It was one hundred percent you . . ."

Silvia's mother smiles. I mistook her for Silvia, but it's her mother. Fortunately the darkness hides the redness spreading across my face, which could explode at any moment into a thousand pieces, like the worst of horror movies.

"Do you want to wait upstairs until she gets back?"

"No, thanks, I'll wait for her here."

"If that's what you want. But . . . sing it to her again."

I sit on the steps outside the front door with my guitar, like a busker asking for money for his art, trying to conceal his shame or some secret in the heart of night. Terminator curls up peacefully at my feet for the first time in his life.

I close my eyes and sing again, almost in a whisper. My fingers play the notes of the melody like a flying carpet, my voice soaring freely across the city rooftops and seizing the stars as if they are the notes of my song, floating in the infinite celestial musical score.

When I open my eyes, a face is scrutinizing me.

That face with caring blue eyes breaks slowly into a smile, like a rusty door creaking open, and from that partially opened door a sudden gush of forgotten happiness inundates me—the kind of happiness that, after Beatrice's death, I no longer felt. It whirls and wraps itself around me, submerging me and whispering to me almost as if singing, "And I will always manage to escape among colors to be discovered . . ."

We hug like two pieces of Lego.

"It seems to me that we match perfectly," I whisper in her ear.

Silvia responds by hugging me tighter. Thanks to that hug I feel my sharp edges, my flaws, my thorns. And I can already feel them softening, becoming gentler and fitting tenderly into her empty places.

Terminator runs around us, forming circles that magically protect us from any possible sorcerer, just like in fairy tales.

And a kiss is the red bridge we build between our souls, which are dancing on the white vortex of life without fear of falling.

"I love you, Leonardo."

My name, my whole name, my true name preceded by that verb in the first person is the formula that explains all things hidden in the center of the world.

They call me Leo, but I am Leonardo.

And Silvia loves Leonardo.

"I'll teach you a game."

"It isn't one of your crazy dares, is it?"

"No, no, it's a game Beatrice taught me. It's called the silence game."

"You mean the one we used to play in junior high?"

"No, no. Listen. You lie side by side in silence. You stay quiet for five minutes with your eyes closed and focus on the colors that appear beneath your eyelids."

On the red bench there isn't much room for two, but by squeezing up close we manage to fit with our faces looking up at the sky. Love is this too: making room for each other when there isn't enough.

Hand in hand, eyes closed and in silence, cell phone set up for the five-minute countdown.

When, during the second minute, I furtively open my eyes and turn toward Silvia, I find her staring at me. I pretend to be angry and, looking at the phone display, tell her there are still at least three minutes to go.

"What did you see?" she asks.

"The sky."

"And what was it like?"

"Blue . . ." *Like your eyes*, I'd like to say to her, but the words don't come out.

As if she has understood, Silvia smiles a perfect smile, without clouds.

"And you?"

"Every color."

"And what was it?"

"A clown . . . and it was you."

"Thanks. How sweet," I say, a bit annoyed.

I had thought of the sky, probably like the most predictable of romantics, but the sky is still the sky. Whereas I appeared in her closed eyes as a dorky circus performer.

Silvia laughs, then she turns serious and speaks without shifting her gaze.

"Harlequin was a boy from a poor family. One day he came home feeling very sad and his mother asked him why. The next day was Carnival, and everyone would have a new outfit even though he would have nothing to wear. His mother hugged him and reassured him. Harlequin went to bed feeling relieved. His mother, who was a seamstress, fetched her basket of colored fabrics, remnants from other items of clothing, and spent the night sewing them together. The following day Harlequin had the most beautiful and original outfit. All the other children were amazed and asked him where he had bought it, but he kept the secret about his mother, who had spent the entire night sewing colored scraps of fabric together—white, red, blue, yellow, green, orange, purple . . . And he realized that he wasn't poor because his mother loved him more than any other, and that costume proved it."

Silvia says nothing for a few seconds.

"Leonardo, you are the most beautiful person of all because you have known how to give and receive love, without holding back. And it has left a clear mark on you."

"It's you who's like that, Silvia."

I stare at the sky in silence, with Silvia nuzzling her face between my neck and shoulder, our hands clasped together like a perfect puzzle. I feel like I can see my skin covered in a thousand squares of colored cloth.

After all, life does nothing but cut you out a multicolored garment, at the cost of endless sleepless nights, nights made of the remnants of other lives and then sewn together.

It's precisely when we're feeling poorer that life, like a mother, is sewing us the most beautiful thing to wear.

First day of school. I wake up forty minutes early. Not because it's the first day of school, but because I've decided to pick up Silvia from her house. I speed off on my new Batscooter (which is a reincarnation of the previous one, but with brakes) in the September air that holds blue inside it, blue like the lucky charm I'm wearing around my neck. I zip between cars like Silver Surfer.

I laugh at everything and everyone, even at the dozy crossing guards and the red lights, who try in vain to stop me. When I get there, Silvia is already waiting for me. She's the punctual one, not me. She hops on my steed. I can feel her hands clinging tightly to my waist. It feels like my life is in her hands.

She's not scared like she used to be. If for no other reason than the fact that I now have brakes. My Batscooter has become a white horse, not galloping but flying over the road. I am alive! I look at the sky and it seems almost as if the moon, still white, is God's smile of approval at what I'm doing. But he soon thinks again when he sees Niko sidling up to me with his devilish look, challenging me to a dare that I cannot refuse. I let him win because I have Silvia behind me, but the smile that Niko and I exchange at the end of the dare is the warmest of handshakes, the reddest of embraces. Things are always so much easier between guys.

First day of school. When I'm sitting next to Silvia, even the school hours seem short, wonderful, and full of life. It's as if the dying universe has been given the blood transfusion it needed in order to breathe again.

As of today I'm going to start writing. I need to write all these things down so I remember them. I don't know if I can do it, but at least this time I want to try. Maybe it's best to use a pencil. No, pen is better. A red pen. Red like blood. Red like love, the ink of the crisp white pages of life. I believe the only things worth remembering are those told with blood; blood doesn't make mistakes and no teacher can correct them.

The white of these pages no longer scares me, and I owe it to Beatrice. Beatrice, white like milk, red like blood.

I stare at the blue of Silvia's eyes: a sea in which to be shipwrecked without dying, an ocean floor where there is always peace, even when a storm rages at the water's surface. And as this sea cradles me, I smile the perfect smile. And without words, my smile says that when you truly begin to live, when life bathes in our red love, each day is the first, each day is the start of a new life.

Even if that day is the first day of school.

Dear Leo,

I am returning your manuscript. I read it all in one go, in one night, and it reminded me of a story about a famous Greek general who, with the aid of only six hundred men who had taken refuge on Mount Parnassus, had to face an immense army of enemies who had surrounded them at the foot of the mountain. Defeat was certain, but the soothsayer of that small army had an idea: he suggested scattering chalk powder over his comrades, over themselves and their weapons.

This army of ghosts attacked the enemy during the night, with the aim of killing anyone who wasn't whitened. The sentries of the huge enemy army were petrified by the mere sight of them. Thinking it was some weird phenomenon, they started to scream and retreat in the middle of the night, pursued by the army of ghosts whose pallor was heightened by the moonlight. The troops were paralyzed with terror, so much so that the six hundred men eventually conquered the battlefield and were left surrounded by four thousand blood-soaked corpses. The blood had also dirtied the armor and the whitened skin of that army of ghosts, and the mixture of white and red appeared even more frightening in the light of dawn.

Leo, at times we fear enemies who are much weaker than they appear to be. Only the white that shrouds them in the dead of night makes them appear mysterious and terrifying. The true enemy is not a soldier covered in chalk powder, but fear.

We need white.

Just as we need red.

Perhaps you don't know that recent anthropological studies claim that, in most cultures, the first words that referred to color distinguished between light and dark. When a language became refined enough to include the names of three colors, the third one almost invariably referred to red. The names for other colors only developed later, after the term for denoting red became common usage, and often the word for "red" has a connection to the word for "blood."

Scholars confirm what you have found out by living. Cultures and civilizations took decades to discover what you have discovered in one school year. Thank you for sharing your discovery with me.

I have limited myself to supplementing parts in which you talk about me and correcting a few subjunctives here and there. Other than that, I haven't touched any of your words. It would have been like touching your life, and I want that to remain intact.

I am proud to have taken part in this adventure and am proud of you.

Your incurable teacher,
The Dreamer

Acknowledgments

Once, a student of mine, despairing over the umpteenth writing assignment I had burdened him with, suddenly asked me, "Sir, why do you write?" I replied instinctively, "To know how it ends." And it always ends in the same way, in writing as in life: with a thank-you.

Someone has said that bad writers copy and good ones steal. I don't know what category the reader will consign me to, but one thing for sure is that both stem from the debt we have toward life and the people from whom we have copied, stolen, or—less furtively—received. Life always has the best copyright: a tireless scriptwriter who turns us into characters ever more capable of love and of loving.

As children we were constantly tormented with the prompt: "So, what do you say?" And we would reply with an exaggerated *thaank youu* that we didn't remotely believe in. As I grew up, however, saying thank you became not just a question of common sense, but perhaps the happiest way of getting by in life.

And so it is:

To my family, from whom I learned that love is possible, always; to my parents, Giuseppe and Rita, who this year celebrate their forty-fifth wedding anniversary; to my incredible brothers and sisters who, with their points of view, add subtleties and nuances to the colors of my world: Marco, the philosopher; Fabrizio, the historian (with Marina and Giulio); Elisabetta, the psychiatrist; Paola, the art historian; and Marta, the architect as well as the author of the photograph of me on the book cover. To these I add Marina Mercadante-Giordano and her family.

To those who believed in this book and helped me to bring it to completion: first and foremost Valentina Pozzoli, unrivaled deliverer of stories, without whom this one would not have seen the light of day. Then: Antonio Franchini, who believed in it from the start with the same enthusiasm I saw in his children as they listened to fairy tales on the terrace known as "Greece"; Marilena Rossi, who knows and loves the characters more than I do; Giulia Ichino and Alessandro Rivali, friends as well as sensitive, honest, and meticulous proofreaders. I would also like to thank everyone at HarperCollins who has worked on the English-language edition, including Daisy Hutton, Amanda Bostic, Becky Monds, Jocelyn Bailey, and Jodi Hughes.

In no particular order to all those who, in various ways and at different times, have played a role behind the scenes of these pages: first-year students (sections A and B) and colleagues at the Liceo Classico San Carlo in Milan; students in Rome, particularly the second years at Liceo Classico Dante; students at Iunior and Liceo Visconti, at the theater group "Eufemia" and at "Ripagrande." Mario Franchina, my unforgettable high school teacher, and Father Pino Puglisi, who one day, when I was in my fourth year, failed to come back to school. Gianluca and Tessa De Sanctis, Federico and Vanessa Canzi, Roberto and Monica Ponte, Angelo and Laura Costa with their families, friends of the "Living Room" and "Delta." Paolo Pellegrino, Rosy from the bookshop II Trittico, Raffaele Chiamili, Sveva Spalletti, Guido Marconi, Filippo Tabacco, Alessandra Gallerano, Paolo Virone, Antoine De Brabant, Michele Dolz, Valentina Provera, Sirio Legramanti, Paolo Diliberto, Giuseppe Corigliano, Sergio Morini, Mauro Leonardi, Armando Fumagalli, Marco Fabbri, Paola Florio, Maurizio Bettini, and my PhD colleagues Emanuela Canonico, Susanna Tamaro, Giuseppe Brighina, Roberta Mazzoni, Lorenzo Farsi, Carlo Mazzola, and Marcello Bertoli, and my neighbor's dog.

And to you, reader, who, from a sofa, beneath the bed-covers, in the street, on a bus, on a red bench, or wherever most takes your fancy, have reached this page and therefore have dedicated your precious time to my characters . . . Thank you.

P.S. In Italy, the rules that govern blood donation by a minor are stricter and more complex than what may come across in the novel. In this context, narrative purpose has prevailed over rigorous adherence to reality.

About the Author

Photo by Marta D'Avenia

Alessandro D'Avenia holds a PhD in classical literature and teaches Ancient Greek, Latin, and literature at a high school in Milan. *White as Silence, Red as Song*, his first novel, was published in Italy in 2010 as *Bianca Come il Latte, Rossa Come il Sangue.* It sold a million copies in Italy, has been translated into over twenty languages, and was released as a film in 2013. Alessandro has since published four more books, the latest of which, *Every Story Is a Love Story*, was published in October 2017.

About the Translator

Tabitha Sowden was born in the United Kingdom, raised in Italy, and is a curious traveler and explorer of cultures and languages. She has an extensive portfolio of Italian to English translation work built up over fifteen years of collaboration with some of the most prominent names in the world of publishing, film production, and design.